The Next Cut

Part Two of
The Barbershop Quartet

A.R. Ryder

ISBN: 978-1-8384993-2-7

The Next Cut

Cara is excited. At least, she's meant to be. Declan, her fiancé, is due in London in a week's time to take her back home, back to Ireland.

She and Declan have been an item for as long as Cara can remember and everyone back home is looking forward to the wedding and the sound of tiny feet - lots of them.

Cara is happy except… she will miss London, her friends, her flat, her job, her youth. But she can cope with all that, she's a strong woman. But then, just as Declan is about to appear, she meets Jack.

And that's where things really start to fall apart…

The Barbershop Quartet

The First Cut
The Next Cut
The Deepest Cut
The Final Cut

ARRyder.com

The
Next Cut

ARRyder.com

Chapter 1: Jack

I'm back where I belong. It's my first day back and I'm a happy man, reunited with my old colleagues, my friends. This is Mac's barbershop, his 'gaff', he's the one in charge, he's my boss. But it's more than that, much more, Mac is my friend, my mentor. He slaps me on the back, 'Welcome back, Jack.'

'Thanks, mate.'

He looks around at all three of us – me, Eoin and Tony. The Four Musketeers he calls us. 'This is how it should be,' he says, a smile on his face, his whiter than white teeth showing through his beard. 'I still want to make Mac the Clipper the best barbershop this side of the river, and you are the guys that can make it happen, we are the coolest of cool, hipper than hip. So, let's make this work, let's cut hair and make it beautiful.'

'Amen to that,' says Tony.

'Let's get to it,' says Eoin in his Irish accent.

Mac opens the shop door and it's all a bit of an anti-climax, to be honest. But there again, it's nine o'clock on a grey, rather dank morning in North London. Tony takes our first customer.

I look around at Mac's shop. I'd only been away for a short while but I was still seeing everything with fresh eyes and, got to hand it to Mac, it's a brilliant space here. It's got what Mac calls the 'industrial vibe': sandstone brick walls with lots of framed photos of cultural icons, like Elvis, Bruce Lee, Marlon Brando, Dolly Parton. And lots of trendy knick-knacks: a baseball bat, a glittery skull that looks like a work of art by Damen Hirst, lightbulbs around the mirrors, a large rosette, ceiling fans, and usually dance music on the stereo that gets progressively louder as the day wears on. It's a great place to work. Men come from miles around, Mac is positively famous in these parts, women too, bringing their boys for their haircuts.

But a few weeks back, I made an error of judgement – I left Mac the Clipper and, shock horror, went to work for Ian at Top Cutz, Mac's rival down the road. I don't even know why I did it, if I'm totally honest, but I did, and I knew I'd made a mistake from Day One. I started the same week as Alice, Mac's girlfriend, soon to be wife. She's an attractive woman but I hated the way Ian talked to her, the way he made her feel.

So I'm back and all is forgiven. Although, is it? I'm not sure about Eoin. It's there in his body language, the way he talks to me. 'So what was it like then, working for Ian?'

'The man's a twat.'

'Huh! I could've told you that, saved you the bother of finding out for yourself. But you never actually asked, did you? Didn't think of asking?'

'I should have, I know.'

We stand in silence waiting for the next customer, when Eoin's mobile rings, releasing both of us from the awkwardness. He talks to the caller in monosyllabic sentences, not sounding overly infused by whoever's called him. A customer comes in, Mr Taylor, one of Mac's regulars, a rotund man who always brings his dog in with him, a runty little Jack Russell called Alby with super short legs and a loud bark.

Eoin finishes his call. 'That was my sister,' he says, even though I didn't ask. 'She's popping by in a minute.'

'Didn't know you had a sister,' I say purely out of politeness.

'Well, you do now.'

'Right.'

This is not going too well. Mac is talking motor racing with his customer, and Tony about the price of diesel with his, the usual shit we talk about on a daily basis. You certainly learn the art of small talk when you're a barber. Football is the biggest topic by far though. If you train to become a barber, you have to know about football, it's an essential part of the job.

Alby the Jack Russell half-heartedly barks at us. Mr Taylor shouts at him to shut up. Eoin pulls a face and the dog wags his tail. Eoin goes down on his haunches to say hello to the hound, while I check my phone. It's then, at that innocuous moment, when the door opens and my life sort of... stands still. For there is a woman of ravishing beauty that it positively knocks the air out of me. Her copper-coloured hair gleams under the lights, strands of which fall across her face, her skin is translucent pale accentuated by the redness of her lipstick, her grey eyes pierce me. She also has at her side, a dog, a black and tan dachshund, a rather sweet looking thing.

'Cara,' says Eoin. '*Dia dhuit*, hello! You were quick. You alright?' He leans in and kisses his sister before bending down and patting the dog. 'Hello, Patch,' he says.

'Here,' she says, handing him a key. 'How are things? There's four of you here. I thought you said—'

'Jack's come back.' He looks over at me. His sister follows his gaze and her eyes lock onto mine, and my heart is exploding. She's wearing a two-tone black and white top beneath a lime green jacket, and she looks fantastic.

'Hi,' I manage to say.

'Hello there. So you're the famous Jack.'

I'm not sure I like this, what has Eoin been saying about me? 'Sure.' I offer my hand.

'Oh, how formal,' she says but she smiles the widest smile and I want to melt.

'Famous?' I ask. 'Or infamous?'

'Oh, a bit of both perhaps.' Her dog woofs at me. 'Do be quiet, Patch. He's a friend's dog. I'm dog sitting for a couple of days.'

'Nice.'

'And this is Tony,' says Eoin, leading her away from me. 'Tony, this is Cara.'

Tony's customer gawps at her in the reflection of his mirror. Tony and Cara exchange a few words but she glances over at me with a look so piercing that my heart soars. Why did she do that? Had I made an impression on her or did she sense I was watching her and wanted to make sure. Heck, I turn away, not wanting to creep her out. Eoin introduces his sister to Mac and Cara compliments Mac on his shop.

Alby, sitting next to Mr Taylor's chair, growls at Patch. His hackles rise. Patch sniffs the air and, unwisely, in my mind, pads towards Alby, his tail wagging. It happens so quickly: Alby launches himself at Patch, there's a squeal and loud growling and yelps and a ball of white and black and tan fur. Eoin shouts and Cara screams Patch's name, Mr Taylor tries to slap Alby but misses. I rush over and instinctively grab Patch by his collar and yank him into the air, yanking him free of Alby's attack. Mr Taylor hits Alby as I cradle the shivering Patch.

'Oh my god, Patch,' shrieks Cara.

'I'm sorry, love,' says Mr Taylor, still berating his dog. 'Is he alright?'

Cara takes Patch from my arms. 'Yes, I think so,' she says. She strokes him and holds him tightly against her chest. 'It's OK, Patch, it's OK now.' Her soothing words help Patch calm down. 'Poor boy, poor Patch.' She turns to me and with that smile that renders me weak, says, 'Thank you, Jack, thank you so much.'

I bow. 'My pleasure.'

'You're a lifesaver.'

Mac and Tony turn their attention to their respective customers while a third customer comes in. Eoin approaches him.

Cara gently puts Patch back on the ground. 'He's too friendly for his own good,' she says. 'Eoin missed you, you know.'

'He did?'

'I know he tries to act all hard but that's just it – an act.'

'He's never mentioned you. Do you live nearby?' I feel myself redden. 'I'm sorry, you don't have to answer that–'

She laughs. 'It's fine, I don't mind. I live on Charlton Road, do you know it?'

'Just beyond the post office.'

'That's the one, number eighteen. But don't tell Eoin I just told you that.'

'No.' I glance over at him but he's too busy settling his customer to listen to us.

'I've been in London for two years already but he's still rather…'

'Protective?'

'Yes, that's right. Protective. Older brother and all that. He means well but it can be a little…' She steps closer and I breathe in her smell, a lovely mixture of candy and cinnamon that leaves me swooning. 'A little overbearing. You two are rather alike, in fact, all four of you are. All beards and tattoos and not one of you under six foot something.'

'I think Mac makes it a prerequisite for working here.'

Eoin calls over. 'Hey, Cara, I thought you said you were in a hurry.'

Cara winks at me. 'See what I mean?' she says quietly. 'Just going, Eoin.'

'You look after that dog now.'

She looks at me. 'It was nice, really nice, to meet you, Jack.'

'And you.'

'And thanks again for saving Patch.'

And with that, she leads Patch away, kisses her brother goodbye and heads for the door. About to leave, she pauses at the door and, turning, throws me a final smile.

And then she is gone and my heart is already aching for her.

Chapter 2: Cara

Hannah, my flatmate, has just made us each a cup of coffee. She was about to leave for work when I walked back in looking flustered. Not wanting to miss out on a story, she decided to hang around a bit and hang work. 'So?' she says. 'What's up?'

'Holy Mother of Jesus, I'm not sure what happened there.'

'What?'

I patted Patch. 'I went to drop a key off with Eoin at his barbershop and...'

'Yeah, I pass it every day on the way to and from work. What about it?'

'Well, I met this guy. Someone Eoin works with, called Jack, and Christ on a stick, he was...'

Hannah's eyes are popping out of her head. 'Yes?'

'Fucking gorgeous.'

Hannah's mouth drops open. 'Cara Smith, you're a soon-to-be married woman. You can't be talking like that.'

'I know. I *know*, Hannah.'

'But what do you mean gorgeous, as in what exactly?'

'Well, imagine, if you will, a cross between some sleek

Hollywood A lister and a… a bodybuilder.'

Hannah puts her hand against her chest. 'Oh my god, really?'

'I mean, talk about the full package: muscles, beard, tattoos and taller than a… a tall thing. Shit, Hannah.'

'But he was a dick.'

'No! That's the thing – he wasn't. In fact, he was rather shy actually, and really polite. He saved Patch's hide.'

'And you reckon he's single?'

I shrug. 'I didn't get that far.'

Hannah slams her coffee mug on the table. 'Right, I'm going there right this minute.'

'You can't.'

'Why? Why not? If he's half as gorgeous as you–'

'Because I saw him first!'

'So what? I'll say it again, Cara, in case you forgot – you are spoken for, girl, you are getting married, remember? So you are out of the equation.' She smiles, a triumphant look on her face.

I sip my coffee while Patch goes and sniffs in his dog bowl, always hopeful that something like a tasty morsel might have dropped into it. I shall miss him when he goes. Hannah's right, of course.

'And, remind me,' she says. 'When's Declan due back? If memory serves, Cara, I think you said he's back, er, tomorrow, was that it?'

I nod. She knows full well.

'So will you be wearing his ring again by that time?'

'Shit.' I didn't even know she'd noticed. Damn it. Declan had bought me a nine-carat diamond and oval-shaped sapphire engagement ring. Very nice and not cheap. I don't always wear it.

'And after all this time away, I reckon he'll be desperate to get his rocks off. Am I right or… am I right?'

'Actually, no, you're not.'

'No? You're joking, right?'

'No, I'm not joking. Declan, he's… well, he's rather old fashioned; he doesn't believe in sex before marriage.'

Hannah looks at me as if I'd grown a beak. 'What the fuck, Cara?'

'I know, I know. It's just… they're a bit traditional where I come from.'

'Hellfire.'

'Still…' I grin at her. 'No harm in a bit of window shopping.'

'Window shopping? As long as you don't touch the goods.'

I sigh. 'No such luck.'

She reaches over and lays her hand over mine. 'Oh, Cara, what am I going to do without you?'

'You'll be fine.'

She glances at her phone. 'Shit, look at the time. It's all right for you – you lady of leisure.'

'Yeah, that's me.'

'I'd better go, I'm late enough as it is.'

'I don't want you going via the barbershop.'

She laughs. 'Trust me.'

'Yeah, butter wouldn't melt.'

After Hannah has gone, I stand up and look out across the street, finishing my coffee. Hannah and I share a second floor flat in this Edwardian London townhouse. We've been here coming up to two years now. We'd never met before moving in but we hit it off immediately. She had a boyfriend until recently when she dumped him for being 'too wet', I think was her expression.

I'd started dating Declan so long ago, I can't remember life before him. He is a good man, an upstanding man, a God-fearing, pillar of the community man. He's educated, has a well-paid job as an accountant and once he's passed his chartership, he'll be earning even more. He is the sort of man who will 'look after me' while I pop out one baby after another. It's what I'm expected to do – by Declan, his parents and my parents. My parents back home in our tiny village to the north of Dublin love him. He can do no wrong in their eyes; he's the son they never had. And now, having completed his first set of accountancy exams, he's coming over to help me move back home. We're getting married in three months' time, a huge rural wedding with a hundred or more guests, hardly any of whom I know, they're all elderly or long-distance relatives or family friends of our parents, hardly any friends of our own. *But I'm happy; I'm looking forward to it.* If I say this enough times – I may get to believe it.

I gave up my job just the day before yesterday having served out my notice. I worked as a publicist for a company that does hair transplants, nothing glamorous but I loved it. I loved the people I worked with and the clients we had, and the pay was decent. But as I'm leaving London and marrying a rich man, I don't need a job any more, not with Declan looking after me. How lucky am I.

And now I'm moving out. The landlady's found Hannah a replacement for me but said Hannah could have the final say on whether she moves in or not.

I'm not jealous that my brother gets to stay in London. My mother and father don't mind that Eoin does whatever he likes, working as a barber instead of getting a *proper* job, a professional job. But not me. It's different for girls, especially small-town, Irish, Catholic girls. I may as well be living in 1955.

I'm not expected to have a job and earn any money of my own; I'm simply expected to have children and bring them up as good little Catholics while looking after and obeying my husband.

Someone passing on the street shouts at an acquaintance. Patch barks.

I need to pop out to the shops and get some groceries in but all I think about right now is Jack. I noticed him the moment I walked into the barbershop. He's a mirror image of Eoin, all three of them are of the same mould, good looking guys all of them. But I'm not sure they realise it – I know my brother doesn't. He doesn't have a girlfriend although I've seen how girls look at him, I know he could if he wanted but I think he likes being single. So Eoin was speaking to me about me getting my stuff from a lock-up he rents, and I tried to concentrate on what he was saying but all the time my gaze kept shifting over to Jack. At one point, he caught my eye and I had to turn away.

And then we had the dog fight. Poor Patch. I call him over and, bending down, stroke him. I dread to think what would have happened to him if Jack hadn't bravely stepped in and pulled Patch free of that beast of a Jack Russell. I thanked him but it was all a bit of a haze, I think I was in shock. I didn't thank him enough. I'm a good Catholic girl, I know the importance of gratitude and saying my thanks. 'A box of chocolates, Patch. What do you think? Does Jack look like the sort of guy who'd appreciate chocolate, do you think?'

Patch wags his tail. I take that as a yes.

Chapter 3: Jack

The day is almost done. It's been a busy day, one customer after another, non-stop. Hardly time to draw breath. But it's been fun, it always is, we've had some good blokes in, lots of banter and jokes and talking shite about football and politics and Covid and Brexit and the rest of it. The sun is still keeping an appearance outside, flooding the shop in a warm, late afternoon light. Mac's turned the stereo down and is bagging up the takings from the till.

Tony left half an hour ago. Eoin popped out to get some chewing gum and I'm just sweeping up the loose curls of hair around my station. I can't stop thinking about Eoin's sister. I think he got fed up with me asking about her, and I wish now I hadn't asked. She said she lived on Charlton Road, and I know it well. At one point I tried searching for her on my phone's Facebook app but Eoin came up to me and I quickly swiped it away, knowing I looked guilty as hell.

So, I've learned a lot about Cara in the last couple of hours – she's twenty-two years old, works in a place that does hair transplants, came over from Ireland two years back and has always lived in the same second floor flat in Charlton Road. But then he tells me the thing I don't want to know – that she's engaged.

I couldn't hide my shock, my searing disappointment. 'Engaged?'

'Yeah. Engaged.'

'Oh.'

'Why are you looking like that, Jack? What's it to you, mate?'

'Nothing, mate.'

He looked at me for the longest time. 'Jeez, you eejit, you've taken a shine to my sister.'

'No, not really, no, not at all.'

Tony, overhearing this, laughed. 'I think you protest too much, Jack.'

So what, I thought? Was it something to be ashamed of? No, Cara is a beautiful woman, it's obvious that she'd be engaged. 'What's he like then?'

'Who?'

'The fiancé, of course.'

'What's it to you? You're gonna invite him round for tea or something.'

'No, just wondering.'

'He's a bit of a twat, to be honest, a *cute hoor*.

'A what?'

'*Cute hoor* – it's Irish meaning… someone who engineers things to their own advantage, gets folk to agree with him, you know?'

'So you're not a fan?'

'Not really.'

It's not much of a victory but right now I'll take anything. So my love rival is a *cute hoor*. Who knew?

'My parents think the sun shines out of his arse though. My

parents and his parents have known each other for ever. I knew Declan when we were kids. He was always the bookish one, the one destined for great things.'

'You've achieved great things,' says Mac from the other side of the shop, cutting a customer's hair.

'Yeah, absolutely.'

That was an hour back. I'm wiping my mirror and tidying everything away ready for the new day tomorrow. We're about to lock up for the day when the door opens. 'Sorry,' Mac calls out. 'We're just closing. Oh? Hello again.'

'Hello.'

Just the one word and my heart stops – that Irish accent. I spin round it's her. Patch is with her, looking slightly apprehensive.

Her eyes dart from Mac to me. 'Can I have a quick word with–'

'He's just popped out to the shops,' says Mac. 'He'll be back in a minute.'

'No, I meant… I meant Jack.'

'Oh?' Mac throws me a puzzled look. 'Yeah, sure.'

Cara comes over. I swear she'll be able to hear the beating of my frantic heart. 'Hello there.'

'Hi. Listen, I…' I spot a blue box of something she's trying to hide behind her back. 'About earlier. I honestly think you saved Patch's life and so… anyway…' She holds out the box. 'These are for you.'

'Oh!' It's chocolate. 'I love chocolate! Thank you.'

'No, thank *you*. From me *and* Patch.'

'Look, I'm just about to head home but why don't we grab a drink in the pub, the White Oak, just over the road.' Shit, I've gone too far, she looks surprised, shocked even. Damn it. 'I'm sorry, you've got a boyfriend, a fiancé even. I shouldn't have asked, I'm sorry.'

'No, it's… it's fine. That'd be good, yeah, why not?' She smiles, a faltering smile. 'Just a drink, no big deal.'

Eoin chooses that moment to walk back in. He sees his sister. 'Cara? You all right? What are you doing here?'

Cara and I both look shifty, our faces red all of a sudden. 'I just p-popped by,' says Cara. 'With a little something for Jack.'

'You what? Why would you be wanting to do that?'

'Because he saved Patch from that horrible Jack Russell.'

I hold up my box of chocolates with a sheepish smile, aware of looking slightly absurd.

Luckily, Alice chooses that moment to come into the shop and divert everyone's attention. 'Hi guys,' she says cheerfully. 'Hi darling,' she says to Mac, giving him a big kiss on the lips.

He hugs her and whispers something into her ear. They're so sweet together, made for each other.

'Right,' says Mac. 'We're all ready to go?'

Eoin and I grab our coats while Cara and Patch wait with Mac and Alice outside next to the door. Mac sets the alarm, then double locks the doors. 'Right, all done,' he says. 'See you guys tomorrow. We're off to try that new Italian restaurant. Nice seeing you, Cara.' We all say our goodbyes to Mac and Alice.

'I'll walk you home if you want,' says Eoin.

'Oh, erm, no, it's OK,' says Cara, glancing between her brother and me. 'It's fine, really.'

Eoin doesn't look happy and I need to step up here. 'We're just popping into the Oak for a quick drink,' I say quickly.

'You what?'

'It was my idea,' says Cara. 'As a thank you for saving Patch.'

'Chocolates and a drink?' says Eoin.

'You can join us if you want,' I say. Why did I say that?

He looks at his sister, then me. 'No, you're OK.' Oh, the relief. 'Thanks anyway.'

He buttons up his coat, raising his eyebrows at Cara in a *I'm watching you, sister* way. He leans down and kisses her, and whispers something. She nods back. 'Goodbye, Patch,' he says, then, without saying goodbye to me or even looking at me, he walks briskly away.

I puff out my cheeks. 'That was awkward.'

'Yes, I'm sorry.'

'No, it's not your fault, it's just… Shall we go for that drink then?'

She smiles. 'Yes, let's. That'd be nice.'

Chapter 4: Jack

'I did tell you Eoin's rather protective of me.'

'You did to be fair. But I didn't think…'

'He'd be *that* protective? I know. Tell me about it.'

Cara and I are settled at a round table in the centre of the White Oak pub. Patch is under the table, so quiet no one would know he was there. It's early so the place is still quiet – just us and a few early evening drinkers. I take several gulps of my frothy beer. Cara's a red wine girl. We share a packet of salted peanuts. A strange part of me doesn't want to talk – I just want to look at her, to have a chance to take in her beauty, that pale, flawless skin, those wonderfully grey-bluish eyes. If anyone had told me this morning that I'd be in the pub this evening having a drink with a beautiful, fair, Irish maiden, I wouldn't have believed it. Yet here I am and I feel like the luckiest man in all London town. I don't normally have a problem talking to people, to *women*, but I feel intimidated by Cara's beauty. God, I'd give everything up for one night with this woman, *everything*!

She asks me what it's like working with her brother. I tell

her all about Mac the Clipper, while she talks about her hair transplant place. 'We sorta have similar occupations,' she says. 'Except you take the hair off while my colleagues try and put it back on again!'

I laugh loudly at that. She buys me a second beer and herself another glass of wine. The pub is filling up now.

Cara tells me about Ireland. I tell her about being brought up in London. We talk about how we survived the lockdowns, and how Mac's business struggled through being forcibly closed for so long. She tells me about living with her flatmate, Hannah, and about Hannah's needy ex-boyfriend. We talk and talk and laugh a lot, and before we realise it, we're onto our third round of drinks and a couple of hours have flown by. I could talk to her all night.

'Eoin and I have a sister,' she says. 'Ava. Older than me but younger than Eoin. She's pregnant.'

'That's nice. When is it due?

'Two months' time. But it's not an easy situation. Her boyfriend fucked off the minute he found out.'

'He did? What a bastard.'

'Yeah. Shame because, up to that point, I liked him and I always thought he was a decent man, you know? Barry was his name. Local boy, so I reckon I'll bump into him next time I go back there, and I'm telling you, he'll regret the day. My ma was really upset. We're very old fashioned over there. The idea of Ava having a baby out of wedlock was bad enough but that was fixable – up to the point Barry fucked off. Now that she's going to be a single mother as well…' She shakes her head. 'My mother liked Barry. Life can be shit at times.'

We sit in silence for a while, sipping our drinks. After a while, I say, 'Eoin tells me you're engaged.' It's not the conversation I want to have but it's the 'elephant in the room', and I feel the need somehow to get it over and done with.

'Yes.'

So, Eoin wasn't lying. At least I know where I stand now – Cara, this heavenly apparition sitting opposite me, is off-limits, I cannot touch her. 'That's nice,' I muster.

'Yeah.'

She's not very forthcoming about this. 'What's the lucky chap's name?'

She smiles at my 'lucky chap' comment. 'Declan.' She twirls the stem of her wine glass, and stares at the red liquid. 'I've known him since we were kids back home, near Dublin.' She says all this without looking at me. 'I'm due to return to Ireland next week.'

'Oh? You mean…'

'Yes, for good.'

'Oh. Right.' Now, it's my turn to stare into my drink. 'That'd be good for you. And for Duncan.'

'Declan.'

'Yes, Declan. Sorry. Makes sense, I guess.'

'Yeah. That's what Eoin was whispering to me. *Remember, Cara, you're an engaged woman,*' she says, mimicking her brother's voice.

I laugh politely although there's nothing funny about any of this, and I'm dying inside here. I don't know what to say so we both sit in silence, staring at our drinks.

'Listen, Jack, I think it's time I headed home now. I'm sorry.'

'Yeah, sure, of course, yeah. No need to apologise.' I'm trying my best here, maintaining the polite facade while inside I'm screaming.

Patch, perhaps aware of his mistress making a move, stirs and pops his head up from under the table. Cara strokes his head. He's proving to be a useful distraction. 'Right then,' she says. We both stand and fumble for our coats and bags, bumping into each other, apologising. Finally, Cara looks at me and it's a haunted look. Then, she shrugs her shoulders and says, 'You can walk me home if you like.'

'If you want.'

'Yes, I do. Don't forget your chocolates.'

We leave the pub, Patch on his lead, and slowly head in the direction of Charlton Road. It's a warm night, the streets are largely deserted. My legs feel heavy. Here I am walking alongside a woman I feel I've known all my life, the most beautiful woman I've ever spoken to, and I so want to stop her right now and kiss her and tell her not to go back to Ireland, not to marry this man called Declan or Duncan or whatever. My heart is breaking as we walk. I feel like a condemned man, walking my last steps, my heart weighed down by disappointment, knowing I have finally met a woman who has stolen my heart yet knowing she cannot be mine and never will be. I glance at her as we walk side by side, Patch leading the way, and part of me is happy that I've met her, that I got to spend a couple of hours in her company, but part of me wishes I'd never laid eyes on her. How easier my life would have been – living in happy ignorance unaware of Cara's existence. Instead, I am fated now for the rest of my days, knowing I have met and lost the love of my love in just a matter of a few precious, life-changing hours.

Patch sniffs at something on the pavement. We stop. 'I've only been in London for two years but God I'm going to miss it. I'm going to miss Hannah, my job, my brother even.' She laughs. 'I'll miss the flat and living in this area and just being in London.'

'Have you missed Ireland?'

'Maybe. To begin with, but once I got settled, not much, not really.'

We're almost there now. Patch cocks his leg up against a lamppost. A girl cycles past and twinkles her bell at us.

'So you don't have a job to go to in Ireland?'

'I wish. I'll try and find something part-time perhaps, a cafe or something, but I know Declan won't like it.'

The more I hear of this man, the less I like him. 'He sounds like a traditional kind of guy.'

'He is that.' She forces a smile of sorts.

'What does he do, this man of yours?'

'He works in property. His dad started the business. Declan's taking up the reins. He's already a rich man. One day, I imagine, he'll be obscenely rich.'

We're outside Cara's flat now. The idea of leaving her now, of saying goodbye, is killing me. 'This is it,' I say.

'Jack, why don't you come up?'

'You sure?'

'Coffee or something. Unless…'

'Yeah, sure.'

She seems to relax, as if asking me had taken some effort. Even Patch wags his tail. She leads me up the stairs to her second floor flat, my hand on the banister. Is it just me or is the air rife with tension and anticipation? She fumbles with her key, trying to unlock her door. She is as nervous as me. Finally, we're in, Patch leading the way. Cara flicks on a switch. 'We've got the place to ourselves. Hannah's out until late.'

Cara leads me through to the living room. She removes her coat while I take in the bright green sofa, the Shaker-style duck shell blue cabinets, the bookshelves, the bronze, domed lampshade. I catch my reflection in the hexagon-shaped mirror. I look too big, even incongruous, like a giant in a dollhouse. 'Nice place you have here.'

I turn around and Cara is standing right next to me. I'm about to step back when she cranes up and kisses me.

Chapter 5: Cara

I don't think he expected me to pounce on him. He must think I'm such a hussy, that I do this all the time. But he doesn't resist. He's a good kisser, manly, strong but not too domineering. I feel myself moisten. It's too much, I can't do this. I am still a virgin, I am saving myself for my wedding night, like the good Catholic girl that I am. Declan too is a virgin, or so he says. I suspect he is not. I swear I have smelt the lingering odour of another woman's perfume on him.

Jack's hand roams down and he gently cups my breast. Oh, it's like a bolt of electricity straight through to my pussy. Oh god, something is taking over me, making me lose control. I want to see his cock. I've never felt like this before. My hands, rubbing his chest, fall to his belt. I'm a good girl, I shouldn't be doing this, but I'm undoing his belt buckle. I've become obscenely desperate. I've never held a penis before, never taken one in my mouth, never even had much desire to, but Christ, right now I want cock! Jack lifts me off my feet, simply scoops me up as if I weighed nothing, and carries me into my bedroom. He throws me on the bed, then kneeling at the end of the bed, pulls down his jeans and his boxers. Quickly, I slip off my skirt. Oh. My God. The size of it. I don't know cocks but even me, in my innocence, knows that this is Big. But what really shocks me is its width and circumference. Is this normal? There's no way my tiny hole can accommodate that much meat. That thing of his will fucking impale me. Fuck, bring it on. My heart is exploding and my pussy is drowning in my juices. I rub myself.

I wrap my hand around Jack's cock and I fear I'm about to have a heart attack. I grip it at the base. It's magnificent; I can't think of another word for it. My tongue slides along the sensitive underside, and I look up to see him staring down at me. 'Am I doing it right?' I ask, my voice rendered husky with lust.

'God, yes, Cara. That's perfect. I could come now, just watching you.'

Shit, he doesn't appreciate the effect of his words. The fact I'm turning him on turns me on a hundredfold. Fuck, what is happening to me? I've lost all sense of control. I suck him hard, my tongue flicking his glorious knob, but only for so long before my jaw aches. He's too big for me. I fall back on the bed. Jack lies on top and kisses me. Quickly and expertly, he slides a sheath on. I feel his dick near my entrance. This is where, thinking of my wedding night, I should clamp my legs shut and say, 'No.' But nothing of the sort happens. On the contrary, I spread my legs open, and, muffled under his kiss, groan the word 'yes' over and over. He circles the head of his cock over my clitoris. I gasp. I swear I've never experienced such intense pleasure. Around and around, setting my nub on fire. I can barely breathe. He guides his wondrous cock down until I feel its tip nudging at my entrance. But he stops there. Why has he stopped when heaven on earth is just seconds away? 'Are you sure, Cara? We don't have to take it so far. It's fine.'

'Don't you dare fucking stop, Jack. I'm saying yes, all right? Fucking yes, yes, yes. I want you. I'll beg you if you want me to.'

He laughs but the laugh dies on his lips as his penis breaches my entrance. I moan, clenching my cunt walls, trying to suck him in. Then, with a guttural grunt, he slides into me. Jesus, son of Mary, that hurts. Sensing me tense up, he pauses. My fingernails rip into his shoulders. He hoists up my tee-shirt and, cupping my breast, sucks on my nipple. Oh fuck, that's good. That's doing the trick, I can feel myself relax, my body falling into the bed, the tension dissipating and my pussy opening. Sensing it too, Jack pushes himself in another inch. I scream but this time from the pain *and* pleasure, the latter getting the upper hand. 'I don't want to stretch you too far,' he says as he switches to the other nipple.

'I want you to stretch me, God, yes. Fucking stretch me, Jack.' I cup my breast for him, making it easier. My eyes glaze over. Now, only now, he slams into me. I arch my back and scream a long and very loud, 'Yessss!' He picks up his rhythm, pumping harder, faster. 'Sweet Jesus of mine, yes, fuck me, Jack, fuck me.' The sweat pours off my brow. I'm coming! Oh my sweet Lord, I'm coming in wave after delicious wave. He hoists himself up on his arms and with his eyes locked into mine, he fucks me hard until he bucks, his whole body juddering as he comes inside me.

Fuck.

I can't believe I've denied myself up until now. Fuck, I never realised what I was missing out on. Is it always like this? Or maybe it's just Jack? Does having an enormous penis give a man a huge advantage on how to use it? I don't know but what I do know is that I'm in heaven and no way is this going to be a one-off experience. Having tasted its delights I am going to want more and more cock – but only if it's as good as Jack's cock.

I should be full of regret already, hating myself for breaking my promise to remain pure until my fiancé put a ring on my finger. But how can I berate myself when everything feels so right and so good. Jack is lying on his side, facing me, a wide smile on his lips. This is not wrong, this is nothing to feel ashamed about; no, this is just perfect.

Chapter 6: Jack

Cara turns her back on me, sitting on the edge of the bed. She bends over slightly and I have to resist the urge to run my finger down the length of her spine. But my frivolous thoughts are soon shattered when I realise she's crying. 'Hey, hey, hey, what's the matter, Cara? What's up?' She's regretting it already, I know she is.

She turns to me, her arms criss-crossed now over her breasts. 'I'm sorry, Jack—'

'No, I'm sorry.'

'It was me that jumped on you. It's my fault, I shouldn't have done it.'

'I'm pleased you did though.'

'I don't want this to end, Jack.'

She reaches for my hand. I take it. 'Nor do I. Finish with him, Cara. Tell him you can't marry him.'

She uses the heel of her hand to wipe away her tears. 'Oh, Jack, if only it was that easy.'

'But do you love him, Cara?'

'Yes,' she says indignantly. 'No. Oh, Jack, I don't know.

Why is this happening to me?'

'What?'

She punches me in the arm. 'You, you great bear. Everything was OK until you turned up.'

'I think you'll find it was *you* that did the turning up.'

'I can't just leave him, Jack. It's so complicated and so much tied into this marriage. His parents, my parents, our family history, our histories, the whole sodding community. Declan and me – we've known each other since–'

'You were kids, yes, I know.' My tone is sharp. She notices. 'I'm sorry. I didn't mean it for it to come out like that. It's just that…'

'Yes?'

'All I know is that I've met you and the thought of not seeing you again is killing me, Cara.' I bite on my knuckle, I mustn't cry.

'Declan will be here tomorrow. He's having his *English* stag do, as he calls it.'

'English?'

'He lived here a couple years too so he knows lots of people here. You know what expat communities are like, half of London's Irish know Eoin and Declan. So, he's having a stag do here in London.'

'Nice.'

'You see – so many people know about us, about the wedding. The honeymoon's booked, the church, the vicar, everything, Jack, everything. I can't just say, *sorry, folks, it's all off, but hey, thanks anyway*. My mother would crucify me. And my dad – he'd come find you, Jack. I'd hate to think–'

'I can look after myself.'

'Yes, I daresay you could. Still, I wouldn't want to be there.'

'No.'

'Can we swap phone numbers? Would that be OK?'

'But if you're going back to Ireland–'

'I know; you're right but… I don't know…'

'I know.'

But before we have chance to exchange numbers, Cara's buzzer buzzes. We both freeze. Patch, sitting in the hallway, barks. 'Bit late for a caller. Shit, it could be Eoin.'

My heart somersaults at that. 'Maybe your flatmate's forgotten her key?' I ask hopefully.

'I doubt it. Jack, put your clothes on. Quickly.' It buzzes again as I grapple with my trousers. 'Hurry, Jack. I'd better get it.'

I hear Eoin's voice come over the little speaker. 'Can I come up?'

'Now?' says Cara. 'You want to come up now?'

'Well, I wasn't calling to make an appointment for a later date, Cara. Jesus wept, woman.'

'Oh, OK.'

'So… are you going to let me in or what?'

Cara glances over at me. I'm half-dressed now – just my jumper and jacket. 'Sure. Come up.' She presses the button, allowing her brother inside. 'Christ, bloody Eoin.'

'He's not going to like this.'

'He's not going to find out.'

'Hey?'

'Hannah's room, Jack. Please, I hate doing this but please, just this time, stay in Hannah's room.'

I want to protest, say it isn't fair, but I know I won't, I know I'd do anything for this woman. I grab my jumper and jacket and close the door to Hannah's bedroom just as Eoin knocks on Cara's front door. Should I sit on her bed, at her dresser, or lie on the floor behind her bed in case Eoin comes in. In the end, I opt to stand behind the door so even if he glances in, he won't see me. I hear Patch barking and brother and sister greeting each other, Eoin asking about Hannah's whereabouts. I can hear her leading him into the kitchen. Cara says she's about to have an early night.

'So you seemed rather taken with Jack earlier, Cara.'

'He's a fine-looking man.'

'And you're a fine-looking woman, Cara, and it was obvious he was smitten with you, but it's not on, you know.'

'It's that why you're here, Eoin? To check up on me?'

'No. I was just on my way back from seeing a friend, so I thought I 'd say hello.'

'Well, you've said your hello, Eoin, and as you can see, I am on my own.'

I slip my jacket on. I can hear the front door opening. Shit, what's happening now? Patch barks again. 'Hi Cara,' says a female voice. 'Oh hi, Eoin.'

'Hi Hannah,' says Eoin.

Shit. Oh shit.

'How was your evening?' I hear Cara ask. Is it just me or can the others hear the tremor in her voice?

'Fine but I'm dying for the loo.'

'Yes, of course. Take your time.'

'You what?'

Eoin laughs at this. 'Take your time? You mad?'

I hear Hannah's footsteps and the toilet door closing and the bolt being pushed in. I can't stay here. Hannah will be coming at any moment and she'll scream on seeing a strange man in her room. I have to leave…

Chapter 7: Cara

This is mad. Eoin's talking about Declan and his imminent arrival in London. Hannah is in the toilet and Jack is hiding in Hannah's bedroom. It's like some situation comedy or a bedroom farce. At least I had the presence of mind to slip Declan's engagement ring back on my finger. Eoin, being a man, probably wouldn't have noticed but it's best not to take a chance. What's Hannah doing back so early anyway? I see her bedroom door inch open. My heart pounds with dread. Eoin will see. He's still talking. 'Eoin, come to the window for a minute.'

'What for?'

'I… I want to show you something. I mean, ask you something.'

Looking slightly puzzled, Eoin gets off his chair and hauls himself over to where I stand at the window. 'What is it, sis?'

'That car, the blue one down there. What is that?' I glance behind and see Jack creeping towards the front door just as I hear the toilet flush.

'Why are you asking me that?'

'I'm thinking of buying a car and I want one like that so…'

'It's a Ford Fiesta, they're not exactly rare.'

Hannah comes out of the toilet just as the front door closes. Patch wags his tail. We've done it! Jack is gone, we got away with it. My whole body sags with relief.

'Did I hear someone leaving?' asks Hannah.

'Do you like Ford Fiestas, Hannah?'

'Do I what? I don't know. Never given it a thought. Why?'

Eoin sits down.

'Oh, nothing, just wondering.'

I sit opposite my brother and I feel quite weak. Hannah and Eoin talk but I can't listen, my brain fogs over. Hannah is laughing a lot, both of them are. If I didn't know them both, I'd say there's a certain attraction between the two of them here. Hannah goes to her bedroom.

Eoin yawns and stretches his arms above his head. 'Well, I'd best be going. Look, Cara, sorry if I come across as the heavy-handed brother and all that, but you know Ma and Pa, they asked me to look out for you. Which basically translates as getting you to the church on time.' He laughs but I don't. It is not a laughing matter as far as I'm concerned. 'She's not getting any better, you know, Cara.'

'I know that, Eoin.'

'We're talking months here.'

'Don't say that.'

He stands and comes to give me a kiss. I see him to the door. He's almost out when Hannah appears at her bedroom door, and she's holding something vaguely familiar in her hand.

'Who is this?' she asks, holding it up.

Oh shit, my stomach plummets. It's a jersey, a blue-striped jumper, and I know exactly who's it is. But I shrug, nervously glancing sideways at my brother.

'What's it doing in my room? Who does it belong to? Is it yours, Eoin?'

Eoin looks puzzled. 'No but…'

'Anyway, Eoin, thanks for popping by–'

'Wait. I… I recognise that.'

'Do come by again. If you get to speak to Ma and–'

'That's bloody Jack's jersey.'

'Who?' says Hannah.

My face turns beetroot-colour in an instant.

Eoin glares at me. 'What the hell is Jack's jersey doing here? Oh shit, he's been here, hasn't he?'

'No, he was just passing by, he–'

'*Passing by?*' He's shouting now. 'What the fuck, Cara? So, if he was just passing by, as you say, why is his fecking jersey in Hannah's room?'

'Because… because…' I look from Eoin to Hannah. I can tell Hannah is feeling bad for me now, that she wishes she hadn't said anything, but it's too late. And I think of Jack, and I think of Declan, and I know I love them both. And I know that's mad because I've only just met Jack, so how can I be in love with him, it's impossible, but even just thinking of him makes my legs turn to jelly.

'Well?' says Eoin as if he was my father, not just my older brother.

Hannah puts her arm around me and I wonder why she's doing that. And it's only then that I realise I am crying.

Chapter 8: Cara

Hannah is making me a cup of tea. Patch is lying on his bed in the kitchen. Eoin stands at the window, looking down over the street. I wonder whether that Ford Fiesta is still there. I'd almost gotten away with it. Silly Jack. Why did he have to forget his jersey, or his jumper, as he called it. He will have realised by now. He'll be panicking and wondering what to do? Whether to wait outside until Eoin leaves and then come back for it or leave it to chance. Perhaps, in his hurry to escape, he hasn't even noticed. I remember the hurt on his face when I ordered him to hide in Hannah's room. Poor Jack. Does he hate me now? He must think I'm ashamed of him. I'm ashamed of myself. When will I see him again, when can I apologise to him and say, no, I am not ashamed of you, my darling, but I am frightened of my family expectations and here, in London, those expectations are contained in one person – my brother.

Hannah hands me my tea. 'Oh, lovey, look at you. I've never seen you look so distraught.' She looks over at Eoin. 'Look, maybe I should leave the two of you to talk.'

Eoin nods while, inside, I'm screaming at her, nooo, don't go, don't leave me alone with him. But I can't say it out loud, and with an apologetic smile, Hannah diplomatically retreats to her bedroom.

I sip my tea, bracing myself.

'So,' says Eoin at long last. He's still at the window, looking outside, as if he's too ashamed to look at me. 'So, are you going to tell me what's going on?'

'We went out for that drink, you know, at the White Oak, and we had a nice time. We got chatting.'

'Yeah, that's how these things usually begin.'

'And he offered to walk me home.'

'I bet.'

'Eoin, stop interrupting me. So, yes, he walked me home, then asked if he could use the loo. So he came up for a minute, Eoin. That was it. No big deal. Maybe he was hot and took his jumper off, and I, thinking it was Hannah's, threw it into her room. I can't honestly remember.' Did that sound as implausible as I fear?

'And that was it? You telling me the truth here, Cara?'

I nod.

'Because if Ma and Pa know you're cheating on Declan, you'd break their hearts. I can't let you do that to them, you know that.'

'Yes, I know. But everything's fine, really. Declan will be here tomorrow. He'll stay a couple nights, have his stag do here, then we'll be off back to Ireland to get everything ready before the big day. So, you see, happy ever after.'

'So why were you crying just now?'

'Because sometimes, Eoin, everything gets on top of me. Everyone expects something from me – to be this fair, pretty bride, to being a wife-to-be and a mother-to-be.'

'Ma and Pa are just excited, Cara. Ma's so sick now, it's the one thing that keeps her buoyed up, you know.'

'But it's more than that, isn't it? They'll be wanting their first grandchild as soon as it's morally acceptable. And they won't be happy unless I produce half a football team's worth of grandchildren for them.'

'Don't you want children?'

'Yes but…'

'But what?'

'On my terms, Eoin, not on theirs or Declan's parents' terms. When I am ready. I don't even know if I want to go back to Ireland.'

'Well, you do because Declan won't want to stay here.'

'Exactly. It's always about what other people want, never what I want. What I want doesn't even come into it, does it? As long as I'm the good dutiful wife, daughter, daughter-in-law, sister. Would you want to go back to Ireland right now?'

'No, of course not. Maybe when I'm older, much older, but not now, no way, I've got my life here now.'

'And I haven't?'

'No, you haven't. That's what you signed-up for when you got engaged to Declan. You *knew* you'd end up back at home, Cara.'

'I want to stay here now, in London.'

'Bit late for that now, isn't it? Or do you want to ditch Declan and start afresh with Jack?'

I don't answer.

'Well? Cara?'

'It's got nothing to do with Jack,' I say when, in fact, it has *everything* to do with Jack.

Eoin looks at me, trying to work out whether I'm being honest with him. He can see straight into my blackened heart,

I'm sure of it. I feel my cheeks redden. I sip my tea, averting my eyes from his. Eventually, he breaks away. 'Right. That's OK then. But you'd better be telling me the truth here, Cara. I like Jack, he's a good mate, but if I know he's hitting on my sister, who is accounted for, he won't know what's hit him.'

The thought appals me but what can I say? I just want him to go now, to leave me in peace.

Luckily, he stands up. 'OK, I'll leave you to it, Cara. I'll see you soon, OK?'

'Sure. Thanks for dropping by.'

'Yeah, right.'

Patch woofs.

And finally my brother's gone and I can breathe again.

Hannah emerges from her bedroom. 'You OK, Cara?'

'Oh, Hannah, what can I do?'

'What do you mean?'

'I'm marrying the wrong man.'

Chapter 9: Jack

Next morning. I'm standing outside Cara's flat on Charlton Road. But she's not in, nor Hannah, her flatmate. It's a bright but cold morning. People are off to work, walking towards the nearest underground station. A woman with headphones on is so lost in her music, she almost bumps into me. She apologises and then scuttles off. I'm wondering whether to leave Cara a note but what would I say? *Hello, it's Jack, I just called to say I love you. PS Have you seen my jumper?* Anyway, I don't have paper or a pen.

The fact is, I'm worried. Last night was the best sex I've ever had in my whole life and now I think I'm in love. I've never felt like this before, about anyone. I can't stop thinking about her. I need to see her again, I want to make love to her again, I want her to be mine. But I know she's not, and she can't ever be, and that hurts, it fucking hurts. And I'm worried that she's forgotten about me already, that she'll never want to see me again. The thought of it rips into me. I can't bear it. She's come into my life like a whirlwind and suddenly it's as if nothing else matters.

So, I don't know where my jumper is. I can't find it anywhere. Did I leave it at Cara's place last night? The thought is an appalling one because what happens if Hannah finds it or even worse, much worse, if Eoin found it. He'd be bound to recognise it and he'd be asking questions. I'd ring Cara but for the fact we didn't swap numbers. We were just about to last night when Eoin came round. And then our evening came to an abrupt end and I had to sneak out like some night-time thief.

I spent the whole night worrying about Cara, whether Eoin gave her a hard time. I could take it if he just gave her a bit of older brother hassle but anything more than that and he'll have me to answer to, friend or no friend, I don't care. I have no right to feel protective of Cara, for I have no claim on her and anyway, in this day and age, she can look after herself. But I *do* feel protective of her, I want to make her my responsibility.

I look at the time on my mobile. I have to get to work. Mac will be expecting me. Problem is, so will Eoin. I wait another minute, hoping that Cara might just turn up. But she doesn't and I have choice but to go.

I get to work just as Mac opens up the shop for business. Eoin isn't anywhere to be seen. I ask Mac.

'He'll be a bit late. Dentist's appointment.'

Damn, I wanted to get it over and done with. Now, I have to wait and it's going to be killing.

'So,' says Mac. 'How was last night with the lovely Clara?'

'Cara,' I correct him. 'It was… I don't know how to describe it.'

'Love at first sight?'

'Yea.'

'Yep, it happened to me, Jack. The moment I laid eyes on Alice, I knew.'

'I didn't believe in love at first sight, I thought it was impossible. How can—'

'But it does happen.'

'Yes, I believe it now.'

'So, what next?'

'She's already engaged.'

'Oh, jeez, is she? That's tough. What does Eoin say?'

'I've not spoken to him since last night but from what I can make out he's over-the-top protective of her and will want her to do the *right thing*.'

Mac slaps me on the back, sighs and wishes me well.

I still need to pick my jumper up for Cara's. I'm not that bothered about it, to be honest, but of course it's always handy to have an excuse to call.

Tony comes in, all cheery as usual. We exchange banter although my heart isn't in it. The first customer of the day is one of Tony's regulars, a young taxi driver. I go to our kitchenette to make the man a coffee with one sugar. More customers come in. Mac cranks up the stereo and the day starts. The sun slants through the door, the postwoman pops in with today's post, more customers come in and everyone is happy. The morning passes quickly.

Finally, come late morning, Eoin returns from the dentists. He doesn't look happy – whether that's because of me or because of something his dentist did, I don't know. He says hello to Mac and Tony but ignores me while he hangs his coat up. I watch him go through to the back where we have the office, the toilets and the kitchenette. After just a few moments, he pops his head round the door and beckons me over. I walk over, feeling condemned, knowing this was *it*.

He closes the door behind me. 'Are you fucking my sister?'

'None of your business, mate.'

He pushes me up against the wall, his hands gripping the top of my shirt. 'No, that's where you're wrong, *mate*. It's very much my business.' His nose is almost pressed against mine. 'Family business.' He glares at me, waiting for an answer I don't provide. 'So? I ask you again, are you–'

'Fuck off, Eoin. I'm not fucking your sister, right.'

He doesn't loosen his grip but maintains eye contact, his eyes boring into mine, looking for the slightest clink that shows I'm lying. I hold my nerve, waiting for the moment to pass. Eventually, he lets go of me and steps back an inch or two. 'You better not be, Jack, because if you are, mate, so help me God.'

Chapter 10: Cara

Declan is due back any minute and I am pacing my flat. I'm wearing my engagement ring. Hannah is in the kitchen, nursing a cup of tea and asking me every now and then if I'm OK, to which I answer every time that I am. But she knows I'm not. I've done the housework, vacuumed and dusted every inch of this flat apart from Hannah's bedroom, wiped every surface, cleaned the toilet and shower. The flat smells of polish and air freshener.

This moment has been building up in my mind for weeks now. Declan and I were last together some six weeks ago. He came for a weekend visit, we went out to a Thai restaurant we like and we spent a lot of time in the pub, drinking. He is a good-looking man, my fiancé, a sexy man, and I was desperate to have sex but no, he is also a conservative, traditional man, and he refuses to have sex before we're married. And now I am deeply worried about that. Will he know, come our wedding night, that I am no longer a virgin, that I gave away that most precious of gifts to a man who is not, and will never be, my husband, to a man I'd only just met. I refuse to be slut-shamed but it's hard to break away from an age-old prejudice. Because whatever I may tell myself a small part of me *is* ashamed. Yet, when I ask myself – would I do it again, I know the answer. Just the thought of Jack makes me go moist between my legs. I think of him all day, I dream of him at night, that wonderfully muscular body, his tattoos, his aura, his smell, his cock, oh god, his huge hard cock. Jack, come give it to me again. I keep having flashbacks to our time together and I want it all again, I want to experience it afresh, again and again. But I must stop this. Declan will be here very soon and he is my husband-to-be, he is the man I have pledged to spend the rest of my life with, I cannot, must not, think of Jack and his cock, and the way he plunged it into me and the way he made me so wet for him, the way he made my nipples so hard, the way he made me come. Oh God, stop, Cara, stop. I want to rush to my bedroom, close the door, lie on the bed and play with myself and imagine Jack's wonderful dick ready to fuck me all over again.

'Cara! I said are you all right?'

Oh hell. My beating heart. 'Oh yes, I'm sorry, I'm just excited, you know.'

'Listen, I'm going to go now.'

'No, you don't have to.'

'But I do. Give you two lovebirds a bit of space.'

'It'll be fine, Hannah. It's not as if we'll be jumping into bed, after all.'

'I know but you've not seen each other for so long, you won't want me here cramping your style.' She gathers her coat and checks her phone. 'OK, lovey, good luck, and I'll see you later.' She winks at me and leaves.

OK, so Hannah is gone, Declan's not here yet, I might have time. I remove my bra and fall onto my bed, pulling my jeans down. I hook my panties to one side and touch myself. 'Oh, heck!' I knew I was wet but didn't realise I was this wet, I'm soaking down there. I lick my forefinger and circle it around my clitoris while imagining Jack on his knees between my open legs, his enormous cock quivering. I cup my breast, a finger flicking over my nipple. God, I wish Jack was here to suck on it. I want to feel the wiry touch of his beard as he takes my nipple in his mouth and sucks hard on it. I run my fingers up and down my snatch then suck my juices off, my eyes glazing over in heavenly lust. I plunge a finger inside of me and yelp loudly. God, that feels good, but it's not enough. I insert two fingers and that's better, circling them around inside me, feeling the walls of my cunt.

Do I have time to take this further? I don't know but it's as if I have no choice in the matter. I roll over and rummage around at the back of the bottom drawer of my bedside cabinet and find Darius, my name for my wonderful rubbery dildo. Darius has been a constant companion to me in the two years since I went into a sex shop off London's Oxford Street and bought him. He wasn't cheap but he's proved good value for money since I use him three, four times a week. I wish it wasn't so but Declan, with his bloody principles, leaves me no option. And Jack, sadly, was a one-off, a beautiful experience never to be repeated.

I rub Darius between my hands for a few moments, warming him up. He's ready. I suck Darius' massive knob, moisturising it, then place it at my entrance. I quickly rub my clit again, making myself even more desperate. Then, slowly, I push Darius in, little by little. My body tenses as I edge him further in. Hell, it feels good. If only this was Jack's cock, not Darius, but it'll do for now. Darius is some ten inches long, but there's no way on God's earth I can take all that, but I slam him in now, as far as I can take it and scream loudly with the ecstasy of it. Darius' other great virtue is his rather unrealistic girth. He stretches my cunt lips wide apart, half pain, half wonderfulness. I pump him in and out, in and out, his girth causing such delicious friction. 'See this, Declan? See this? This, you idiot, is what you're missing out on. My red, wet cunt.' Maybe, just maybe, if it hadn't been for his reluctance to take my cherry, I wouldn't have given it away to Jack. 'Your fucking loss, Declan,' I say aloud as my hand speeds up Darius' pumping. 'And Jack's gain.'

My body is glistening in sweat, my hand is a blur as Darius dives in and out of me, getting faster, causing such friction, taking me to my climax. I call Jack's name as I come, my body juddering, waves of pleasure wracking my body from top to bottom.

And I am done. Oh my god. My chest heaves as I catch my breath. Darius drops from my hand, rolls off the bed and lands with a heavy thud on the carpet. Gee, that was good, I needed that, I was so tense. I'm still panting breathlessly, my shirt around my throat, my bra and panties on the bed, when the buzzer rings.

Chapter 11: Cara

'God, it's good to see you again, baby,' says Declan. 'I've so missed you.'

'And I've missed you too, baby.'

We have a long, intense kiss.

I'd almost forgotten how good looking my fiancé is! He has these dark, come-to-bed eyes and a neat growth – halfway between a stubble and a beard. He hugs me for an age and it feels good. He smells of his musky aftershave but I feel so self-conscious – can he smell the sweat on me, can he smell my juices? I only had time to throw on my clothes when he arrived, pressing the buzzer downstairs. If I had time, I would have had a shower.

'That ring looks good on you, baby. Nice sapphire that, isn't it?'

I twist the ring around my finger, smiling. 'Yes, I love it.' And to be fair, I do! 'I never take it off.'

'Should think not.'

I offer him lunch but he says he's eaten and anyway, he wants to save himself for dinner tonight, the Thai restaurant.

So I make him a tea while asking lots of questions, like how was the flight, how is he, how are his parents, how's his job going?

He's been here before but he looks round the flat as if he'd never seen it. 'Nice place this. Cosy and all that.'

Yeah, more's the pity I've got to leave it behind and that I've already finished my job. But of course I don't say this. He always seems a little uncomfortable here, not just in my flat but here in London. He lived here for a while, built up his career, added lots of experience to his CV and made friends – lots of friends. People always seem to flock to Declan, he's got the famous Irish charm, and people, men and women, love him. That's why he's probably one of the few men ever to have not one but two stag parties, a London one and a Dublin one. I don't ask him about it because I don't really care, if I'm honest.

I take a chair and sit opposite him at our little Formica kitchen table. He glances at our vase of fake flowers. They need dusting – I missed that bit. He's still talking about himself. He pays me the odd compliment but he doesn't ask me anything – about how I am, about how I feel about giving up my job, about anything. 'Have you seen my mother?' I ask, dreading the answer.

He takes my hand. 'She's not looking good, baby. You'll see for yourself tomorrow.'

I take my hand away and sigh. My poor ma.

'I'm telling you, baby, I can't wait for you to get home.'

'Oh? Really?' If you feel that desperate, just take me now. Throw me on the bed; I'd be up for it. Why wait, Declan, why wait?

'Jesus, yes. I can't organise the wedding, can I? And there's only so much you can expect your ma to do. No, we need you.

The bridesmaids are waiting, and the florist, the caterers, and God knows who else.'

'Right. Of course. Silly me.'

'And the house. It's looking tired, you know? It needs a lot of decorating. I could get some professionals but it's not cheap, so you might as well do it all, baby. After all, you'll have the time now.'

'Won't I be too busy with the wedding?'

'Delegate, baby. Delegate. My ma's itching to lend a hand. And your sister. Just bring them on board, tell my ma and Ava what they need to do and by when. They'll thank you for it.'

'But I want a job, Declan. A proper job, like I had here. Jobs are a lot easier to get back home. I mean–'

'Baby, baby, stop, just stop now.' He reaches over the table and takes my hand. 'You'll be too busy to work.'

'But that's it, Declan. If I get myself a job, I'll be able to pay for the decorators myself because, let's face it, they'll do a professional job, much better than I could hope to do.'

'No. We can't allow that. You'll do a fine job. I don't want strange men in the house while I'm out at work all day.'

'Strange men? What do you mean? Don't you trust me, Declan?'

'It's not that, baby, I trust *you*, of course I do, but the idea of men in my house, or *our* house, seeing you all day, eyeing you up…' He shivers as if someone's just walked over his grave. 'It's disgusting. No, I've made up my mind, delegate as much of the wedding as you can to Ava and my ma, while you get on with the painting. Three months. There're not too many rooms, you'll have plenty of time to get it all done, then, once we're married–'

'*Then* I'll get a job.'

He glares at me. I know I've annoyed him. I want to hide

behind the fake flowers. 'Please, Cara…' Oh, I'm Cara again, no longer baby. 'Stop pissing me off, will ya? We've agreed on this–'

'Have we?' You agreed on this, I think, but I certainly did not.

'Yes, we did, we bloody did, you know that.' I've riled him, he's trying to control himself but he's truly annoyed. Astonishing, twenty minutes and we're already arguing. 'You won't need to work. I'll need you at home. I earn plenty–'

'Not enough to pay for decorators.'

'It's not the money, I told you. Anyway, enough now. You are not working when married to me. End of.'

'How is Ava? Have you seen her?'

'Ava? No, I've not seen her.'

'OK, just asking. And what about that bastard Barry? Have you seen him?' He shakes his head. 'Hmm. He's probably keeping a low profile after walking out on Ava and the baby.'

We sit in silence for a while and my thoughts drift, as they always do now, to Jack. He wouldn't talk to me like this. He'd have more respect for me, for women generally. I can't believe I'm allowing myself to be talked to like this but I've never answered Declan back, not even when we were children. Maybe if I had back then, I could now. But it's the fact that his opinions represent everyone I know back home, even my own parents. They love Declan. He'll look after me, they think, keep me on the straight and narrow. I was a bit too much of a tearaway when I was younger; Declan will prevent me from making a tit of myself. Of course, I wasn't a tearaway, I simply had a personality.

'Do you want another cup of tea?' I ask once the silence becomes unbearably awkward.

'No but I tell you what, I'm tired. I had an early start. Had a couple of things that needed doing at work before I went to the airport. Can I lay my head on your bed for half an hour?'

'Sure, baby.'

He both stand. 'It's good to see you again, baby.' He puts his arms out and I step into his embrace. 'I need a couple days off, I reckon.'

'Sure.'

We part. 'I can't wait to marry you, you know.'

'I know.' He raises his eyebrows at me and I realise he's expecting the same back. 'Me too.'

'Right. Bed. Will you be OK for an hour?'

'What? Yes, of course. I'll just… I'll watch some TikTok.'

'Well, if you want to rot your brain, sure.' He stretches and yawns. 'I'll be right as rain in an hour.'

'You go. Have your rest.'

He leans over and kisses me on the cheek. I keep my smile fixed as he lugs himself over to my bedroom, closing the door behind him. I breathe out. I'm exhausted already; it shouldn't be this hard. I sit back down, puffing out my cheeks, but then he immediately reappears again and I know from his stormy expression that he's not happy.

'What's this?' he demands.

'What?'

'This!' He holds up my dildo by its base.

My hand goes to my mouth. 'Oh my god.'

'I found it on the floor next to your bed. And, Jesus, Cara, it's still wet with…' He screws up his face with disgust.

I walk over, taking Darius away from him, my face burning with shame. I hide it behind my back.

'That's gross, Cara. It's wet still, for God's sake. When did you…? No, actually, I don't want to know.'

'I'm so sorry, Declan.'

'You should be. I'm appalled that my wife-to-be should degrade herself like this. Throw it away.'

'What?' No, I can't. I can't throw Darius away. For fuck's sake, he's been more of a boyfriend to me in the bedroom than you have. If only I had the courage to say that out loud. Instead, I stand there, knowing I look panicked, like a rabbit caught in the headlights.

'I said throw it away,' he shouts. He returns to the bedroom, slamming the door behind him.

I look at Darius, feel his hefty weight in my hand, and I know there's no way I can put him in the rubbish bin. But where to hide him? I look in the bathroom but there's nowhere to hide a ten-inch dildo in here! The kitchen? Back of one of the cupboards? Possibly but Declan could easily stumble across it again. Then I have a fabulous idea, a place where Declan would never look. I carefully hide Darius beneath the large pack of frozen peas in the bottom drawer of the freezer. The thought of my juices freezing amuses me.

Well, that was some reunion. Although, if I'm honest, I'm not that surprised. We always end up fighting sooner rather than later. Still, I need a fecking drink. I need wine and I need it now! There's half a bottle left over from last night. What a relief! I half fill a tumbler and sit down again at the kitchen table.

I raise the glass. 'Welcome back, Declan,' I say before swigging the first mouthful, relishing the moment the alcohol hits my bloodstream.

Chapter 12: Jack

I'm so desperate to see Cara again. It's like an ache within me and there's nothing I can do about it. I can't stop thinking about her. I'm becoming obsessed. I've stopped talking at work. I just get on with the job, trying not to talk to the customers, because all I want to do is to think of Cara and remember our brief time together. Eoin and I are hardly talking anyway, not since the man threatened me. Cara doesn't seem like the sort of woman who needs an older brother to protect her; she's quite capable of thinking for herself. But Eoin likes to play the Big Man. I can stick up for myself, Eoin doesn't intimidate me, but I know I need to tread carefully here. It's all a bit delicate.

After work, I hurry over to Charlton Road, to Cara's flat. The night is drawing in, the streetlamps are already on. I spy a fox watching me, his eyes illuminated by a streetlamp. Foxes seem to get braver by the day in these parts. Always on the prowl. I stop outside Cara's flat. I can see the lights are on. She must be at home. I ring the buzzer and hear her voice and my heart skips a beat. But she sounds hesitant. 'Come up, but you can't stay, Jack. Sorry.'

I take the stairs two at a time, such is my keenness to see my darling. She's waiting outside her flat for me, on the landing. She smiles on seeing me but I can see it's an uncertain smile.

She glances back at her door before throwing her arms around me. Oh, her smell, I breathe it in, relishing the moment. 'I've missed you, Cara.'

'I've missed you too. God, I can't tell you how much.'

This is music to my ears. 'I hated having to sneak off last night.'

'Me too. I felt so bad for you. I'm so sorry about Eoin. He's…'

'Don't worry, let's not talk of him. How have you been?'

She hesitates a moment. Then, standing on her tiptoes, she whispers the single word into my ear: 'Horny.'

I laugh. 'Seriously?' She shushes me, glancing back again.

'I want you to take me to bed again, Jack, and I want you to fuck me,' she says, emphasising the last two words in a growl. 'My fiancé's here.'

'Shit.'

'I know. I feel the same.'

'I don't understand.'

'It's a long story.'

'I'd better go then.'

'I'm sorry.'

'I mean, I'd better go for good. There's no point, is there? Might as well cut our losses now and say our goodbyes.'

'Don't say that, Jack; I can't face it.'

'What choice do we have?'

She looks down and the sadness radiates from her every pore. How I'd like to take away that sadness, to make it all better again, but I can't, it's beyond my power. So why prolong the agony? Why make it worse for each other? I feel awful, my heart is dying within me. The thought of letting her go from my grip, of never seeing her again, it's too much to bear. 'Can I have my jumper back?' I don't need it, but it's a way to provide a focus and to lessen the pain, if that was even possible, of our imminent farewell.

'I'll go get it.' She understands, I'm sure.

She's only gone a moment when I hear a man's voice, an Irish accent. I hear Cara say the words 'Hannah's boyfriend's jumper'.

Cara reappears at the door. She hands me over my jumper, all neatly folded. 'Here you are.' She pulls a face which I don't quite understand.

'Thanks.' I'm about to leave, a stone where my heart used to sit, when the man appears next to Cara. 'Hey, Hannah's boyfriend, come in a minute.'

'Well, no, I mean, I wouldn't–'

'Come in, man, come in.'

And so, against my every instinct, I do.

We go through to the kitchen, the three of us. 'So, how long have you been going out with Hannah?'

'Oh, erm…' Cara, hovering behind her man, is holding up six fingers and thumbs. 'About six months.' I know from Cara's expression, I've said the wrong thing.

'Really? Last time I was here, six weeks ago, wasn't it, baby? She was still going out with that other fella, what was his name?'

'I mean, six *weeks*, not months. Sorry.' I hit the side of my head. 'Brain fog.'

'Oh, right. She doesn't hang around, does she? Out with one, in with another. Fancy a drink?'

'Me? No. No, thanks. I won't hang around.'

'Places to go and people to see, eh? So what is it you do, then, mate?'

'Oh, I work as a barber.'

'Oh right. Like my future brother-in-law.'

'Yeah, of course. Eoin. A good man.'

'Yeah, I've known Eoin for years, and Cara, since we were kids. Isn't that right, baby?' he says, twisting around to see her. Cara smiles. 'So, why the need to rush off, mate? Don't you want to see your woman?'

'Oh, yeah, but… you know.'

'No.'

'Got an appointment. Anyway, Cara, good to see you again and er, nice to meet you…'

'Sorry, should have said. The name's Declan.'

'Declan. Thanks for the jumper and all. I'll see myself out.'

'Hey, Jack, what are you doing tonight?'

'Tonight? Nothing.' As soon as I say that, I know I'm going to regret it.

'Brilliant. In that case, you are cordially invited to join me and a couple of mates for my stag do.'

'Oh?'

'Yeah, I knew you'd be pleased! Just a pub crawl around the locals. We're meeting in the White Oak at eight. Seriously, be there, it'll be cool.'

I can't think of anything worse. 'Erm, OK. Sure. Right, I'd better go.' I scuttle off, pleased to escape. But just as I open the front door, there is a woman there, a key in her hand. 'Oh, hello,' she says, surprised to bump into me. She sees the jumper in my hand. 'Oh, are you—'

'Hannah,' calls Cara from the kitchen. 'I told Jack you'd be back any minute and to wait for you.'

'You did? That's nice but what for?'

I whisper to her. 'I'm your boyfriend right now.'

'You are?' she whispers back.

'Yes. Cara said.'

'In that case.' She steps into the flat, removing her coat. I follow. 'Oh, hi, Declan. Welcome back.'

Hannah and Declan hug. Cara looks at me, shaking her head. How did we get into such a situation?

Hannah though steps into her role. 'Shall we retire to my room, Big Boy?'

'Why, yes. Good idea.'

Declan winks at me. 'Don't forget. The White Oak.'

'Sure,' I say. 'I'll be there.'

Ensconced in Hannah's bedroom, I place my folded jumper on Hannah's bed and, going up to the window, I look out onto the shared garden out the back. Hannah removes her shoes. 'So, you're my boyfriend now? Why's that?'

'It's a long story.'

'Am I helping Cara out?'

'Yes.'

'That's all right then.' She looks at me carefully, her hand on her hip, her eyes going from head to toe. 'Are you that barber she mentioned? Works with Eoin?'

'That's me.'

'Oh yeah. I pass your barbers on my way to and from work every day. Cool place. As it is, I could do with a boyfriend. Honestly, I've not had a shag in weeks, and you'd fit the bill very nicely. So, come on, get your kit off.'

'I want to be Cara's boyfriend.'

'Oh? You do? A lot of men do, she's a beautiful girl but… as you can see, she's thoroughly accounted for. So you might as well have me instead. Honestly, I give great head. My blow jobs are legendary, apparently.'

'Oh, it's very good of you to offer but–'

She laughs loudly. 'Listen to you, *it's very good of you to offer.* So polite. What are you like? Gosh, you're serious, aren't you? So how do you propose making Cara yours when she's about to be married to her childhood sweetheart?'

The thought of Cara with Declan just on the other side of this door is making me feel ill. 'I don't know yet but I'll think of something. I have to.'

Hannah nods her head. 'Well, good luck with that, Jack.'

Chapter 13: Jack

The White Oak is heaving, far more so than it usually is at eight at night. It takes me a minute to realise why – they're all Declan's friends. They've taken over. Declan doesn't even live in this city and he has more friends here than I've ever had, a man London born and London bred. How does he do it? I've already worked out he's an obnoxious, self-centred human being. He sees everything and everyone through the lens of his self-gratification. So how can he have so many friends? An old Bruce Springsteen track is playing. A couple are singing along. The pool tables are all being used. Someone bumps into me – a woman with a yellow shirt. I say woman but she's barely eighteen, I reckon. Twenty at a push. 'God, sorry, mate,' she says. 'My fault. Are you alright?' She's attractive for sure, long blonde hair, green eyes, very slim. She looks up at me and smiles.

'Yeah, I'm fine, thanks.'

She squints at me. 'Do I recognise you?'

'Me? I don't think so.' I see Declan propped up at the bar. He catches my eye. 'Hey, Jack.' he calls. 'Come over.'

'Excuse me,' I say to the girl in yellow.

'Maybe catch you later,' she says as I make my way over to the bar.

Declan shakes my hand, a real manly shake. 'Glad you could make it. You alright there?'

He seems fairly drunk already. He introduces me to a few of his friends but it's all slightly embarrassing because he can barely remember anyone's names or he mixes people up. Somehow, we get through it. 'Here,' he says finally. 'Let me get you a drink. What you having, mate?'

He buys me a pint of Guinness. I thank him. I raise my glass. 'Here's to you and Cara. Cheers!'

'Yeah, thanks, mate. Cheers!'

'So,' I say, wiping the line of Guinness froth off my moustache. 'How's it going with Cara?'

'Oh. fantastic. She's a babe, she really is. I can't wait to put that ring on her finger though. Too many blokes look at her, so I want to stake my claim, you know. She's a virgin, would you believe. In this day and age. A virgin! Never been touched. Rather quaint, don't you think – saving herself for me. She thinks I'm saving myself too. Don't like to tell her that I've had so much sex that I've literally lost count of the number of women I've bedded.' He laughs loudly at this.

I try not to show it but I'm shocked. How can he lie to Cara about such a thing? It's a monstrous thing to tell the person you're about to marry. 'How do you know she's not lying to you?'

His eyes narrow and I know he resents the suggestion. 'Because she wouldn't fucking dare, that's why. But listen, once we're married, I plan to let her make up for lost time, if you know what I'm saying.'

The thought of the two of them having sex leaves me a little nauseous.

Declan continues. 'I want to have loads of kids. We're going to bring them up in a nice area of Ireland, where we live, not too far from Dublin, not some shithole like this place.'

'It's not so bad around here,' I say, aggrieved that he should call my home, the place of my birth, a shithole.

'You're joking, right? The unemployment, the crime, the drugs? And it's so crowded around here, it's like the Black Hole of Calcutta, too many people, too many immigrants, if you ask me. Nah, no way I'd want my kids to be brought up here.'

'Nothing wrong with that. I was born and brought up around here.'

He looks at me then laughs. 'Yeah, exactly! No offence, mate, but…'

He doesn't get to finish the sentence because someone calls out his name. Apparently, he needs to buy some more drinks. He turns to me and asks if I want another. I hold up my nearly full pint and tell him I'm fine, thanks all the same. I turn around, leaning against the bar. I catch sight of the girl in yellow. She sees me and raises her stemmed glass at me from across the pub. I nod curtly in return. Madonna's playing now on the jukebox, appropriately enough, the song, *Like a Virgin*.

'Hello, Jack.'

Oh, that's a voice I know – it's Eoin. Declan sees him too and offers to get him a drink – another Guinness. The two men talk for a while. 'I'll not be staying long, I'm afraid,' says Eoin. 'But I wanted to pop in and say hello to my future brother-in-law.'

Declan claps Eoin on the back. 'Appreciate it, mate. Here's to our families, soon to be the most powerful force in our part of Ireland.' The two men clink glasses before Declan gets distracted and disappears.

'What's that about?' I ask. 'The most powerful force in your part of Ireland?'

Eoin takes a gulp of his drink. 'That's the idea. Our families own everything for miles around. We've always been in competition, so why compete when you can join forces and blow the rest of the competition out of the water?'

'Like a marriage of convenience?'

'Exactly that.'

I absorb this for a while, drinking back my Guinness. 'Do they even love each other?'

'Guess so. You'd have to ask them. But it's not the most important thing here.'

It's all a bit too much to take in. First, Declan lying to Cara about his virginity and now this – that the marriage is little more than a transaction between two warlords. It's grotesque. The landlord turns up the volume. Beyonce is now playing. 'Who are all these people?' I ask Eoin. 'How can he have so many friends when he was only here for five minutes?'

'Friends?' Eoin laughs. 'They're not friends, Jack. They're just hangers-on, acquaintances at best, more like gold diggers and the like.'

Of course, that's why Declan had such difficulty remembering anyone's names earlier.

Eoin could see the look of incredulity on my face. 'It's true,' he says. 'They're here because they know Declan will buy them drinks all night long but not one of them will be bothered to make it all the way over to Ireland for the wedding. Too much expense and too much bother. He's not worth the effort. But tonight, while he's paying for the bar, he's their top man. They're twats, every last one of them. And Declan either doesn't care or he's too stupid to notice. I'm not sure which is worse.'

We watch Declan for a while, talking to a woman with dyed red hair and a black, crossover, low top. 'Do you want him as your brother-in-law?'

'Not really but it's not about me. He'll provide for her, for sure.'

'Only financially.'

'True. But it's not my problem, is it? I'm staying put in London. It's Cara's choice and if he's good enough for her, then that's enough for me.' Eoin finishes his drink. He slams the empty glass on the bar and belches. 'Right, I'm off, mate.'

'Really?'

'He won't care. Look at him, he's already past caring. And I don't want to hang around seeing him make out with some brassy lass.' He slaps me on the back. 'Good to talk to you again, Jack. I'll see you at work, yeah?'

We fist bump. Eoin leaves.

I drink my drink slowly, still at the bar. I suddenly feel awfully sad for Cara, to be ensnared in this ridiculous relationship, with a man who cheats and lies to her, who buys his friends, who uses her as a bargaining chip. A man happy to yank her away from where she's happy with no thought for what she wants. But hey, Cara will put up with it all because it's all about family, isn't it, being seen to do the right thing, living up to other people's expectations. She has a role to play, and play it she will – unless I can save her, unless she wants me to help save her. I'll do anything to help her but it's up to her whether she wants to be helped.

I decide I don't want to be here any more. Several of Declan's friends seem to have quietly slipped away. I doubt Declan has even noticed. I look over and my mouth drops open in shock. He's kissing the woman with the red hair, and his hand is visibly disappearing up her top. How can he do that, here, on his own stag night?

Like Eoin, I'm not hanging around to witness any more of this. I'm out of here. I gather my jacket and head for the door when I almost bump into someone. It's her again – the girl in the yellow top. 'Off so soon?' she says with a flick of her blonde hair.

'Yeah.'

'Why don't you stay a bit longer? You can buy me a drink, if you want.'

'No, you're OK, thanks,' I say. I barge past her, ignoring the look of hurt on her face. But I didn't ask to be accosted.

As soon as I step outside into the cold evening air, I've forgotten about her. I can only think of Cara, of how I can save her from making the biggest mistake of her life.

Chapter 14: Cara

'He wouldn't have it,' says Hannah. It's gone half past nine, and we're in the kitchen. I'm already thinking of going to bed. Declan will be out enjoying his stag go with his London friends and colleagues, drinking and dancing the night away and God knows what else. Jack should be there too. I dread to think how they're getting on, they're both so different.

'Sorry, Hannah, what did you say?'

She's rummaging around in the fridge, looking for something to eat having just got back from a late shift at work. 'Your Jack.' She throws me a worried look. 'Sorry, am I allowed to call him that? Perhaps not, since you're spoken for. Anyway, Jack told me I had to pretend to be his girlfriend so I said, let's do it properly and go to bed.'

'You what? Hannah!'

'Oh, come on, Cara, you know I'm desperate. I even told him I give great blow jobs–'

'Hannah, for love of Jesus, what are you like?'

'Keep your hair on, lovey, he turned me down flat. He said… I want to be Cara's boyfriend.' She says it in a feeble attempt at impersonating him but fails miserably.

'That's how he sounds, is it? Did he really say that?'

She giggles. 'I'm not making it up, Cara, that's what he said. Turned down a legitimately excellent five-star blow job because *I want to be Cara's boyfriend*. What sort of man is he? How about mac and cheese?'

I gaze out of the window seeing a crow preening on the apex of the roof on the house opposite. 'He's a very fine man.'

'Yeah, but, Cara, in case you need reminding. . you already have a very fine man so would you mind… just let Jack know so he can move on and move into my bed. Got it? Oh, I can't be bothered to cook. I thought we had a couple of ready meals?'

'Have a look in the freezer.'

A second crow joins the first, this one with a worm hanging from his beak, as if showing off to his mate. Hannah rummages around in the freezer.

'Veggie lasagne. That'll do. Plus some frozen peas and… and maybe a very large and thick dildo for dessert.'

'Oh shit!' I jump out of my chair.

'I mean, what the hell, Cara?' She holds Darius up by his base, the same way as Declan had, but while I'd felt ashamed then, and deeply embarrassed, this time it's just funny.

'I had to hide it.'

'In the frigging freezer? Er, why?'

'Decan found it and he wasn't happy. Told me to throw it away.'

'He bloody didn't.'

'Huh huh, he did. And I thought, I'm not chucking Darius out, he's served well over the years.'

'*Darius*? You're serious?'

'Good name as any, don't you name your vibrators?'

'Well, now that you mention it… So, instead of putting him in the recycling, you decided to hide him in the freezer.'

'Yep.'

'Fair enough. I have to say if any man ever makes me decide to choose between him and my favourite dildo, then I know who I'd be choosing.'

'Yeah, but Declan is better at doing the washing up.'

'And that's just as important, I guess. Well, I suggest we pop Darius back in his hiding place.'

The buzzer rings. We both freeze. 'Who could that be at this time of night?' asks Hannah.

'It can't be Declan; it's too early.'

Hannah goes to answer the door. 'Hello?'

'Hi, it's Jack.' My heart has just done a cartwheel. 'Is Cara in?'

'Hang on.' She covers the speaker with her hand and whispers, 'Are you in?'

'Hell yes.'

Hannah speaks into the speaker. 'Hell yes.' She presses the button, allowing him up.

Moments later, he's there, slightly out of breath, having run up the stairs. And Jesus wept, he looks all man, my God.

Hannah positively swoons as she welcomes him into the flat. I stand and greet him with a kiss. 'Aren't you at Declan's stag?'

'Yeah, I was. But I slipped away. He doesn't know me and he's got lots of his friends there so he won't miss me.'

Hannah clears her throat. 'Do you want me to…'

'No,' I say. 'You've not eaten yet. We'll go, give you some peace. Come, Jack.' I lead him into my bedroom, closing the door behind us. We stand a foot apart, looking at each other. God, how I want him, and I can see his longing for me in his eyes, he wants me just as much as I want him. One moment, we have a foot of space between us, the next, we're kissing. I groan, muttering his name. I so want him but I know I can't, we shouldn't be doing this, not with Declan now staying here. But the heat rises within me and I know I am powerless to resist.

His hands reach down into the back of my jeans. Quickly, I unbuckle the belt, allowing him easier access. His hands squeeze my buttocks and I squeal with delight. Jack kisses my neck and my arousal shoots up like the mercury in a thermometer. We remove our clothes in record time, stripping down to our underwear. We stagger to the bed. I fall on my back and prop myself up on my elbows. He pulls apart my thighs. His finger hooks my panties to one side. He gasps on seeing my engorged snatch. He groans as he dives in, planting a kiss on my clitoris. I screech with lust and joy. He sits up and removes his boxers. I groan loudly on seeing the length of his wonderfully long penis and the sight of his heavy balls, so full of cum, and all of it for me. I squirm with hot anticipation. He falls back onto my wet cunt, parting my lips with his lips, dragging his tongue over my bud. Gently, he eases a finger inside me, causing me to cry out. He climbs up on the bed and, propping himself up over me, kisses me. I taste my juices on his lips and my belly flips. He uses his hand to guide himself to my entrance. His helmet gently breaches my sex. We both hold our breaths, then, after another moment's pause, he drives his cock in hard. I screech and arc my back. 'Oh God, Cara, this is so perfect.'

'Yes, fuck me, Jack, fuck me.' Oh, my cunt lips are stretched by the thickness of his dick inside me, his massive girth. And I am in heaven. He's planted himself so deeply within me, throbbing, plunging again and again. I hold up his arms, fearing he might tire, and feel the strength of his biceps, the tendons in his muscular forearms. I look him in the eyes as he pumps into me. 'Go on, Jack, go on.' I want him to cum, to spill his wondrous seed. 'Jesus, mother of Mary, that feels so good, so fucking good.' He's so big inside me it almost hurts. He's splitting me in two, impaled on Jack's wondrous penis. He pushes himself up further, changing the angle of his cock as it slides in and out of me, causing greater friction. I dig my fingernails into his buttocks, pushing them even harder into me. I feel the pressure rising, the intensity of his pumping, and I know he's not too far off. His pectorals flex, which I find such a turn on. His chest is glistening with sweat. I wrap my legs around him, squeezing his body tighter to mine. He maintains his glorious, rhythmic thrusting. His eyes bore into mine. He needs this, he needs me, only me.

'You OK, Cara?' he whispers.

'Christ, never better, Jack, as long as you keep pounding me.'

My urging has the desired effect and his thrusting intensifies. I feel him rubbing on my clit and oh, Jesus, the joy of it, it's making me come. My body is juddering as the climax washes over me. My eyes glaze over and I know I'm whimpering.

My limbs flop. But my mind is still racing. I know this will be my last time with Jack; it won't happen again, it's impossible. Declan will be back soon, pissed from his night out, still refusing to fuck me because of his oh-so laudable sensibilities. So I have to enjoy this and milk it for all its worth. I may have come but I'm not finished yet. 'Come, Jack, it's time for me to go on top.'

Chapter 15: Jack

Watching Cara come like that was amazing. It made my balls ache and my heart beat with longing. She doesn't appreciate just how stunning she is. I've had my fair share of women over recent years but nothing like this; Cara is in a league of her own. I love the fact that I made her come, it's so life-affirming and such a turn-on. Cara's tongue touches the tip of my dick. Oh, I let out a deep groan. Then, braver, she takes more of me, gulping me down until my knob hits the back of her throat. She licks the undershaft of my cock, from top to bottom, while cupping my balls. 'Is this OK, Jack? Am I doing it right?'

She has to ask? 'Oh, honey, are you doing it right? Fuck, yeah!'

I take a fistful of her hair and groan yet louder. Does she know that if she keeps this up for much longer, I'll cum? My cock seeps precum. She rubs her finger over it and sucks it off her finger. Fuck! She sucks on me again and glances up at me, her eyes ablaze with lust. Oh, jeez, the sight of Cara with my cock in her mouth, bulging in her cheek, is almost too much.

It's all I can do to hold myself back from exploding in her mouth.

She climbs on top of me, gently lowering herself on me, impaling herself on my engorged dick. She is still slick and ready for me. She lets out a little cry and starts moving straight away. She leans forward slightly, allowing her tits to fall forward and swing in time with her thrusting. It's a fantastic sight! I start pumping from beneath her. We reach a coordinated rhythm, me pumping her from underneath, Cara riding me on top, cupping her breast and pulling on her nipple. She leans forward, still cupping her tit and runs her nipple along my lips. 'Suck me, Jack, suck me.' I can't hold back a second longer, a strangulated noise escapes my mouth as my spunk gushes out from me, pounding her until every last drop is gone.

She falls off me, laughing. Discreetly, I remove my condom. We lie on the bed catching our breaths. 'I'm sorry,' she says. 'I shouldn't have pounced on you the minute you walked through the door.'

'I'm rather glad that you did.'

She laughs at this. We rearrange the sheet to cover our modesties.

'Poor Hannah, she'd have heard everything, and she's gagging for it. *I haven't had a shag in weeks*,' she says impersonating her friend's voice. 'She told me she offered it to you. You know she wasn't joking? If you'd said OK, she'd have dropped her panties for you in an instant.'

'I thought she meant it; I wasn't sure. But I would have refused anyway. I've only got eyes for now, Cara.'

'Stop it.'

I prop myself up on one elbow. 'Cara, please don't marry him. I know you say you have to and I understand all that, but it's your life here, not anyone else's.'

She gazes up at the ceiling, unable to look at me. 'Jack, I've not told you the real reason.'

'What do you mean?'

'My mother's poorly, Jack. As in she doesn't have long to go. The doctors are saying six months tops.'

'Shit.'

'She's always loved Declan. He's the son she never had. She even said that she'd die happy if she lived long enough to see me and Dec marry. You see?'

'I do but…'

'But what, Jack? Yes, you're right, it's wrong of me to marry someone for the wrong reasons but even you'd have to admit here, that's one hell of a pressure. What can I do? What would *you* do?'

I have no answer for that. My whole body seems to deflate. I'm beaten, I see that now. This beautiful woman I've so fallen in love with can never be mine. I want to tell her about Declan's lies and his deception but I can't bring myself to do it, I don't want to add to her misery.

'My sister and I, we're both under pressure. I need to be married and she needs to have this baby before Ma dies. As it is, Ma's distraught that Ava is going to be a single mum. Bloody Barry.'

Her mobile pings. She reaches over and reads the text. 'Shit, he's on his way back.'

'Already?'

'Jack, you have to go.'

She's panicking. I have no choice but to get up and throw my clothes on. 'Cara, I still haven't got your number…'

'Not now, later. Hurry, please, Jack.' She's put on her dressing gown and is now rearranging the bed so it looks used but not quite so ruffled.

Part of me wants to defy her, to stay put and face Declan, man to man, tell him he's not wanted here any more. But I don't want to upset Cara further. I can't believe I'm having to do this, it's akin to a cold shower. One minute we're in the delicious throes of passion, the next, I'm being kicked out onto the streets. It hurts. I can't pretend otherwise, it bloody hurts. Damn Declan.

I follow Cara out. I see Hannah in the kitchen using her tablet. Cara and I stand, feet apart.

'So I guess this is it,' I say, trying my best to appear composed when inside my heart is breaking.

'I'm so sorry, Jack. I never meant for this to happen.'

'But it has,'

'I didn't mean to…'

'Hurt me?'

'No. Nor myself,' she adds.

She hugs me, standing up on tiptoe. I could quite easily lift this girl off her feet, throw her over my shoulder and walk out of here. Instead, we kiss for what seems like an age, and when finally we part, I see that she's crying. 'I'm sorry, Jack.'

I turn and leave. I can't bear to stay a moment longer, it's killing me.

I close the front door gently behind me and start walking quickly down the street. I want to stop and turn around, to see whether Cara's watching me from her kitchen window. But I can't. I keep walking, my head down, hands in pocket, my heart shattering in a million pieces. My mind cannot process what's happening here, what has happened. A few days ago, I didn't know of Cara's existence, then she walked into my life and turned it upside down. Now, no soon as I have fallen head over heels in love with her, I'm leaving her, never to see her again.

I'm just turning the corner onto the high street when I hear my name being called. I turn around to see Declan running towards me, a smile on his face, apparently happy to see me. 'Hey, Jack, mate. How's it going?'

'Just going home. I'll see you.'

'Hang on a sec.' He looks unsteady on his feet. 'You left early, mate. Although, to be honest, most did. Didn't matter though, not once I met the lovely Eileen.' He hiccups.

Is he talking about the woman with the red hair? 'I don't understand – why do you need to cop off with some random woman when you've got Cara waiting for you at home?'

He laughs. 'Gee, come on, man, don't be so naive! It's nothing against Cara, fuck no, Cara's great. But you know, a man has his needs, and Cara refuses to have sex until our wedding day, so what can I do?'

'Doesn't it make you feel like a shit head?'

He puts his hands out as if defending himself from attack. Maybe he is. 'Whoa, whoa, mate. Don't you fucking talk to me like that. Who do you think you are?'

'I don't know, *mate*. But someone who knows where the lines of decency are drawn.'

'Gee, trying for a sainthood, are ya? Saint Jack of Shit Town.' He laughs at his own joke, before spinning around and heading off.

I want to run after him and smash his face in, remove that self-satisfied smirk off his face for once and for all. But I don't. I watch him zigzag across the road, heading into Charlton Road, heading back to Cara. I clench my eyes shut and allow the tears to come.

Chapter 16: Cara

So this is it. The day I leave London for good and return to
Ireland. I love Ireland, Ireland is in my blood, but the thought
of leaving London behind is killing me. It's like I'm throwing
away the last two years of my life – I've said goodbye to my
job, a job I so enjoyed and which earned me good money, now
I'm saying goodbye to my lovely flat and my lovely flatmate.
Hannah is standing in the kitchen, leaning against the
windowsill, tears in her eyes. I wish she'd go out, leave me
alone. I love her dearly but her presence is making everything
worse. Instead, I tell her that I need to go out – I need to go
to the post office to post something off. She offers to go for
me, but I refuse – because I'm *not* going to the post office, it
is a lie.

And so, ten minutes later I am standing at a bus stop on the
other side of the high street from Mac the Clipper. It's a cold
but bright morning. I can see them all in there: my brother,
Mac, Tony and… Jack. They're busy, each one is with a
customer and I can see another three or four sitting in the cosy
armchairs waiting their turn. They look happy, the four of

them, happy in their work, enjoying the banter with their customers and with each other. Jack looks so handsome and so strong. My heart is breaking – just seeing him there. I want to go in and say goodbye just one final time. But I can't. We've said our goodbye, why make it worse, why make him suffer. I find a handkerchief in my jacket and wipe the tears away.

A bus comes. People get on it. 'You getting on this, love?' says an elderly gentleman with a walking stick.

I shake my head, not trusting myself to talk.

'Whatever it is that you're crying about, love, it will pass.' He winks at me. 'Trust me.'

'Thank you.'

He gets on the bus, sprightly despite the walking stick, and shoots me a final glance before the bus doors close on him. The bus moves on, and Mac the Clipper is visible to me again, Jack cutting a young man's hair.

'Goodbye, Jack. I shall never forget you. Goodbye, my love.'

*

I return to the flat. Hannah is vacuum cleaning. She doesn't hear me come in and jumps on seeing me. We both laugh. It's nice to laugh. I feel some of the tension draining away. Not much but a little. My cases are all packed and waiting next to the front door. I step into my room and it feels so empty and sounds so echoey. It's horrible. I've had a blast these last two years here. I shall miss it so much. The thought of moving back to my childhood bedroom fills me with dread. Yes, I had a happy childhood but it doesn't mean I want to return to it. But my mother needs me. She needs me. I repeat this to myself over and over – my mother needs me. It's not fair of me to hide away in London, ignoring her illness, allowing my poor sister to take all the burden and the strain of a sick mother. I look out of the window and look down on the street, such a familiar scene. But today I'm seeing it for the last time and it's something else I'm going to miss. I've been back to Ireland several times in recent months. Ever since I got that initial phone call from Ma telling me the worst-case scenario had come to pass – that her cancer was malignant, it was spreading and had become terminal. There was nothing the doctors could do, she told me. So, I've been back and forth to Ireland, seeing Ma, holding her hand, talking to Ava, my very capable and lovely sister. Eoin has visited as well but not so frequently as me. And when he does return, it is the return of the prodigal son, the boy who can do no wrong. Let's hang out the flags and the bunting, yay, Eoin is coming home! I am being petty, I know that. But today, of all days, I'm allowed to be petty, truculent, bad-tempered, whatever. But I also know I have to be all smiles and loveliness when, at any moment, my husband-to-be comes to pick me up.

The buzzer rings. It'll be Declan. Hannah answers it – it's not Declan. 'Come on up,' says Hannah.

'Is it Jack?' I ask, barely able to contain my excitement. 'Is Jack here?'

'No, that's not Jack, that's Eoin.'

Oh. Blast!

He comes up. If he's expecting another flag-laden welcome, he'll be disappointed.

Hannah waits for him, although I don't see why. He hasn't come to see her.

'Hi, Eoin, how's it going?' she says the second he steps through the door.

Eoin looks a little taken aback by Hannah's gushing welcome. 'Yeah, sure. Fine thanks.' He looks at me. 'What's up, sis? Why the long face?'

'Oh, isn't that a cue for a joke about a horse?' says Hannah.

No, I think, it's a cue for you to fuck off. But I don't say that. Is she flirting with my brother?

'No, I'm fine. All fine!' I say as chirpily as possible.

'So where is he?'

'Due any second.'

Sure enough, the buzzer rings again. 'Oo, it's like Piccadilly Circus,' says Hannah to Eoin. She bloody *is* flirting with him. This time, it is Declan. Seconds later, he's upstairs with us. He looks surprised to see all of us in the hallway, especially on seeing Eoin.

'Quite the welcome committee,' he says, shaking Eoin's hand.

'I wanted to see my little sister off,' says Eoin.

'Don't worry, mate. She's in safe hands now. I'll look after her.'

'Not sure she needs looking after.'

'Oh, she does, mate.' Declan taps the side of his nose. 'Trust me. But don't you worry, I'll keep her in hand.' Turning to me, he says, 'Everything ready then? The Uber's waiting outside. Shall we go?'

So, this is truly it then. Between them, Eoin and Declan carry my meagre belongings downstairs to the taxi.

Hannah and I look at each other. 'I'm so going to miss you, lovey,' she says. 'Keep in touch, yeah?'

We hug. I squeeze my eyes shut, trying not to cry for I fear if I start, I'll never stop. 'Hannah, can you do me a last favour?'

'Of course, lovey. Anything.'

I give her the letter I'd written just an hour or so ago, now sealed in an envelope with Jack's name on it. 'Can you give Jack this?'

'Sure but why not just give it to your brother. He'll see Jack before I will.'

'I don't want Eoin to know.'

'Of course. Sorry, being a bit slow there. Don't worry, Cara. I'll make sure he gets this.'

'Goodbye, Hannah. Look after yourself.' And with that, I drag myself away from the flat and down the stairs to the taxi, a silver-coloured Kia, waiting outside.

I hug and kiss Eoin goodbye. Declan holds the taxi door open for me, showing off to Eoin that he's an old-fashioned gent. I wave goodbye to Eoin as the car draws away.

Declan immediately starts up a conversation with the driver which is fine by me because I have no energy or desire to speak for a very long time now. The car comes out of Charlton Road and turns left into the High Street. This means we'll be passing Mac the Clipper very shortly on the left. Sure enough, the car gets stuck behind another car and has to halt right outside the shop. I can see straight in, and there he is… Jack. He's standing at the window, clear as day, drinking a coffee. He looks miles away. Our driver beeps his horn and swears at the hold-up in front of us. A woman with a boy holding a blue balloon on a string walks in front of the shop, blocking my view of Jack for a second. Then Jack looks up and sees me. It takes him a second for it to register and when it does, his hand goes to his mouth as if he is trying to stifle a cry. The car inches forward, just as Jack goes to the shop door. Is he coming out? Is he going to stop me from leaving? The excitement of it all. I'm terrified. But then, at that very moment, the traffic clears, the driver puts his foot on the accelerator and we're off. I turn in the seat. Jack is out on the pavement, running to catch us up. Declan is totally oblivious to what's happening. The car is speeding up and Jack, running like mad, can't keep up. He falls over a wheelchair but keeps going. I glance ahead – a big crossroads with lots of traffic lights. Ours is showing green. It needs to turn red, oh God, let it turn red…

Chapter 17: Jack

Mr Chichester has never been a man generous with his tips. I finish his haircut and he says he's delighted with it, that it makes him look a whole lot better, but obviously not quite enough to warrant leaving me a tip. He bumps into Eoin who is returning from wherever he went, muttering under his breath. Whoever he's just spoken to obviously didn't impress him very much. Mac asks him if he's alright but he just grunts and doesn't answer.

No more customers at the moment, although I'm expecting one in twenty minutes or so. I go through to the kitchenette to make myself a coffee. It's been quite a busy morning but nowhere as busy as I would like it to be. The busier I am, the less time I have to think because I know today, right now, the woman I love is leaving me, leaving London and going far, far away. And it hurts, it really hurts. I feel as if someone's stomped on my heart and is refusing to let go, maintaining the pressure all the time, causing this continual pain. Nothing will alleviate it except time, the slow inexorable passage of time. I take my coffee and return to the shop. Eoin, on his phone, ignores me.

I stand at the window watching the world go by, the sun shining. An old woman pushing a shopping trolley accidentally slams it into the back of a younger woman looking at the display at the estate agents. They fall over themselves apologising to each other. A man walking his cocker spaniel has to pause while his dog cocks his leg up against a bin. I envy these people being able to go about their everyday business without this weight pressing down on them. Mac creeps up behind me and puts his massive hand on my shoulder. 'It's difficult, isn't it?'

'Yeah.'

'I wish I had the words to help but I don't. No one does.'

'Who was it that said it is better to have loved and lost than not loved at all?'

'Alfred Lord Tennyson, I think. He knew what he was talking about.'

'Yeah.'

Mac squeezes my shoulder then returns to work.

Did Tennyson know what he was talking about? Did it count when that love lasted so little time? We hardly had time to get to know each other and yet I knew it was love, the real thing, that burned in my chest. Yes, of course I'm happy I met Cara, she changed my life, but to what purpose? Our love had so little time that actually I think in this case, Mr Tennyson is wrong. I wouldn't be feeling like this if Cara hadn't turned up in my life only to then disappear from it so soon after.

A man passes our shop window shouting into his phone like a loudmouth. A car beeps its horn. A mum and little boy pass, the boy holding a blue McDonald's balloon. The car beeps its horn again. What's causing the commotion? Oh Christ, it's Cara, I can see her in the back of that car, the silver

Kia Picanto, Declan sitting next to her. She's looking straight at me. Fuck! The coffee mug slips from my hand, landing on the floor with a loud smash. I run outside but her car is moving again. I'm not thinking, I just know I want to pull her out of that car, to drag her away from that man. I call her name but, too late, the car pulls away, picking up speed. I run like I've never run before, zigzagging around people on the pavement, jumping over a dog, almost crashing into someone in a wheelchair. 'Cara! Cara!' The car is way beyond me now, approaching a junction controlled by a traffic light. I know this crossroads – the lights stay red for ages. If the light turns red, I'll have enough time to catch her up. I stop, catching my breath. Please go red, please go red, please…

*

The day passes slowly. I just want it to end now, I just want to go home, get into my bed and not wake up for a long time.

Finally, it's six o'clock. I'm heading out of the door. Usually, I hang around and help Mac lock up and have a chat about what we're doing tonight. Often, we arrange to meet at the White Oak. But not tonight. I don't even want to talk. But just as I'm leaving, Hannah appears.

'Jack. Hello,' she says, out of breath. 'I was hoping to catch you. Oh, hi, Eoin. How are you?'

'Yeah, I'm great, thanks, Hannah,' says Eoin in an uncharacteristically soppy voice. And the two of them start talking about… about nothing, just going round in circles, as if caught in their very own mating game. Is something going on here? Somehow Hannah has reduced big, gruff Eoin to a simpering, giggly teenager. How has she managed that? I clear my throat with a loud cough. It does the trick. But she looks awkward, glancing between Eoin and me. Eventually, Eoin,

Tony and Mac say their goodbyes. Hannah watches Eoin head off. 'Is there something I can help you with, Hannah?'

'Oh yes. Sorry, Jack. I've got something for you.' She rummages around in her little shoulder bag and produces a blue envelope. 'Cara asked me to give you this.'

My heart speeds up. Thanking her, I take the envelope, my name written clearly on the front.

'I know she liked you, Jack. She liked you very much.'

And with that, she turns and leaves.

I look at the envelope, wondering whether to open it now, standing at the shop door or wait until I get home so at least I can read it in comfort. But the pull is too strong. I can't wait that long. Hastily, I rip the envelope open, pulling the letter out. It's a blue, A5-sized sheet of paper, folded into two, just a few lines. I start to read…

Dear Jack,

I'm so sorry this had to end like it did. I'm so pleased to have met you. I wish we had longer together. I shall never forget you.

All my love,

Cara. xxx

That was it. But what else did I expect? Her telephone number perhaps – I still didn't have it, damn it. Anyway, what else could she write? It said it all, really. I looked up at the sky, the grey clouds scudding by. I shivered and buttoned my coat up to the top. I folded the letter back and returned it to its envelope. It was time to go home.

But just as I'm about to leave, someone says hello to me, a woman's voice I vaguely recognise. Yes, I recognise her but can't think why.

'Hey, we met last night, didn't we? At the White Oak.'

'Oh yeah, of course.' It's the girl with long blonde hair, in the yellow shirt although now she's wearing a dark green coat, certainly stylish.

'Do you work here? In the barbers?'

'Erm, yeah.'

'Oh cool. Anyway, nice to see you again. Catch you at the pub maybe.'

'Yeah sure.' She disappears into the crowds, leaving me feeling slightly unnerved. Did she really just bump into me? Anyway, I don't want to think about her. I reach into my back pocket, making sure Cara's letter is still there.

Satisfied that it's safe, I finally go home.

Chapter 18: Cara

Despite the turmoil raging through my heart, it is good to be home again, to breathe in that pure Irish air. The taxi drops us off outside my parents' home. We live in a large, detached house on the outskirts of a village, some ten miles west of Dublin. It's a pretty area, very rustic, very slow. Declan helps the driver bring all our luggage inside while I race inside to be greeted by my cheerful dad. He gives me a big hug and tells me how lovely it is to have me home for good. I inwardly wince at those last two words but I hide it with a little laugh, and he doesn't notice.

'How's Ma?'

'Go see for yourself, love. She's been looking forward to this day for a long time. But listen, Cara…'

'Yes, Pa?'

'She'll be over excited by seeing you and it'll tire her out. She'll say I'm fussing but be aware of this.'

I rush upstairs, excited to see my mother after all this time but nervous at the same time. She has such high expectations of me on the romantic side, always has done. Even as a young girl, she used to say things like, *Of course, darling, you won't have to worry about money because with your pretty looks, you'll easily find a young man to look after you.* And fairly soon, that generic 'young man' transmogrified into a specific young man: Declan. My parents knew Declan's parents, and they adored Declan. They could not envisage a better match for their 'princess' than young Declan, the boy who 'one day will be a very successful and rich young man'.

I knock on Ma's door. I hear her frail voice telling me to come in.

She's in bed, her arms out, ready to embrace me. My heart stops for a moment. She looks that much older, more fragile, sicker than before. This illness is weakening her. I hadn't realised it was so bad. I want to fall in her arms but she looks too delicate. I hold back the tears; I don't want to upset her. So, I lean down and kiss her. Her skin is so very pale but she's put some make-up on. It's not necessarily for my benefit; my mother is one of these women who, every single morning, always put her 'face' on, regardless of whether she was going out or not. She pats her bed, tells me to sit down.

She takes my hand, her grip surprisingly strong. 'Oh, Cara, my beautiful girl, it's so lovely to have you back. I hated you being in London, with all those crowds.'

'I was fine, Ma. Really, I was. I loved it in London. It was exciting.'

'You say that but you never know with big towns. Anyway, I'm so relieved you're back now.' She squeezes my hand. 'So happy. This is where you belong, Cara.'

I can't help but think of Jack, wondering what he's up to this very moment. 'It's nice to be back, Ma. So, tell me, how are you feeling?'

She tells me. It's not good but she's remarkably sanguine

about it. How does she do it? I couldn't be; I'd be a wreck. But my mother is a believer, she has a strong Catholic faith. She strongly believes that our time on Earth is inconsequential compared to the greater life that awaits us. Life on Earth is but a phase. But, like she says, she has two beautiful daughters, one pregnant although regrettably single, the other about to be married. Her greatest wishes are to be around long enough to see me married to Declan and to meet her first grandson. How can I let her down; how can I not marry Declan?

*

The following day, Ava comes to visit. She is big! Yet she still has a good two months to go before the due date. We both go upstairs to sit with Ma for a while but, remembering Pa's words, not too long – we mustn't tire her out too much.

Ava had a boyfriend, albeit briefly, and the swine buggered off the minute Ava got pregnant and, being a good Catholic girl, she point blank refused to have the pregnancy terminated.

Downstairs, Pa fusses around us like an old mother hen. Declan pops in and chats for a while. Declan and Ava have always got on. Is there anyone in my family whom my fiancé hasn't managed to charm?

Tonight, I'm going to Declan's house for dinner with his parents. They can't wait to see me, apparently. Everyone is happy, so bloody happy. And the happier they are to see me, the worse I feel. It shouldn't be like this.

'Have you thought of a name yet?' I ask Ava once Declan has gone and Pa is outside messing around in his shed, which he is wont to do, especially when two or more women are gathered together.

'Oh yes, but…' She winks at me. 'But it's all a secret.'

I want to ask her so much more, like how is she going to

cope with bringing this child up by herself now that Barry's fucked off, a single mother at the age of just 23. I want to ask whether she's seen Barry since he upped and deserted the minute she announced she was pregnant, greatly upsetting my poor mother. I want to ask whether Barry's going to help her financially. But she's just arrived, I can't launch into such big topics.

'Fancy going on a walk? A bit of fresh air.'

'Yes, let's.'

Fifteen minutes later, we are ambling along a path that cuts through a woodland, the wintry sun slicing through the trees. After all, Ava is several months pregnant so we have to take it gently. 'So, how's it going, Cara?' she asks, her hands holding up the weight of her belly. 'I'm guessing you're not overjoyed to leave London behind?'

'No, it's fine,' I say, gazing into the distance.

'Really?'

'Yes. I'm happy to be back.'

'So why are you biting at your thumbnail?'

'Oh.' I wasn't even aware of doing so. I stop dead. I bite my lip, trying to hold it back and for a moment I think I might succeed but then Ava rubs my back, and the tears come.

Ava takes me by the hand and leads the way out of the woods and onto a small park, where we sit on a bench. We sit in silence for a while, watching a dad and his son playing with a Frisbee. Their dog, a Jack Russell, runs between the two of them, barking and jumping at the Frisbee. The dog reminds me of the first time I met Jack, the day he saved Patch from that man's Jack Russell. 'Right,' she says. 'We're not moving until you've told me everything.'

'I can't, Ava. Mum is dying, I can't do it to her.'

'Do what, Cara? Do what exactly? Cara, there's someone

else, isn't there? You can tell me, Cara. I won't judge. Look at me, the situation I've got myself in. I'm hardly in the position to judge anyone else, am I?'

I laugh at that and have to wipe my nose with the back of my hand.

'So what's his name, Cara?'

'Jack. His name is Jack…' And so I tell her. I tell her everything. How I don't want to marry Declan, and that somehow we ended up in this situation where it's simply expected. And Ma's deteriorating health means I can't say anything, but all I want to do is run back to London and into the arms of Jack. By the time I'm finished, I'm a snivelling wreck. Ava is going to hate me; she's going to resent me for wanting to throw away a perfectly good relationship when she has nothing. But she doesn't. She puts her arm around me.

'What do I do, Ava? Tell me what to do. I know I have to marry Declan.'

'What? To fulfil everyone else's expectations?'

'But it's not just that. Ma's dying, Ava. I can't–'

'No. *No!* It's *your* life, Cara. You cannot marry this man if your heart isn't one hundred percent into it.'

'Really? Do you really think that?'

'Fuck, yes, Cara,' she shouts, drawing the attention of the man with the Jack Russell. 'Jesus, son of Mary, you only have the one life, you can't fuck it up just because other people think you should, and yes, even if one of them is your mother on her deathbed.'

'So you will help me?' I ask, conscious that my voice is as quiet as a mouse.

She squeezes my hand. 'Bloody right I will. I'm your older sister, Cara and I'm going to help you sort this mess out for once and for all.'

Chapter 19: Jack

I'm not sure whether coming to the White Oak to drown my sorrows is necessarily a good idea. But I'm here and it's fine so far. Mac and Alice are here, all loved up. Gee, they seriously can't keep their hands off each other and I'm not sure whether it's making me feel better or not. The song, Every Breath You Take is playing on the pub's stereo system.

'You're suffering, mate, aren't you?' says Mac. Alice, sitting the other side of Mac, looks across at me with pity in her eyes. It's kind of them, it really is, but I don't want pity.

'I've been better.'

'If you want to take a couple days off work—'

'No, it's fine. Thanks anyway but work is good.'

'Like a distraction,' says Alice. 'I can understand that.'

'Is Eoin causing you any hassle because I can always have a quiet word with him.'

'Nah, it's fine.'

'Why don't you go after her?' says Alice. 'Like Mac did when he came up to Keswick.'

The two of them look at each other, a knowing look passes

between them. She takes his hand. It's sweet, so nice to see. They are so in love.

'Alice is right,' says Mac. 'You need to make a stand, let her know how you feel about her.'

'Yeah, you're probably right. I should.'

Tony approaches and sits with us. He starts telling us about the game of pool he's just lost. He seems most put out because he lost to a woman but 'to be fair,' he says, 'she was bloody good.' I tune out.

Cara's letter is in my back pocket. I've not stopped thinking about it. I've read it a hundred times or more, I could recite it word for word. *I wish we had longer together. I shall never forget you.* She'll be in Ireland now, near Dublin, with Declan and her family. I wonder how her mother is. She must be delighted to have her daughter back.

Tony goes to the bar – it's his round. The song Only Love Can Break Your Heart by St Etienne is playing.

I remember my father dying three years ago. He too died slowly. And it was hell seeing him go through it. He too dearly wanted to see me in love and settled. He would have died a happy man if I'd given him a grandchild. And I would have loved it too. I've imagined the scene many times since, holding a baby in my arms, my wife at my side, and presenting the baby to my father. But it wasn't to be; I failed him. Not that he blamed me because it wasn't my fault but I guess it's something deep in all of us – to see our bloodline survive and thrive.

And that is why Mac and Alice are wrong – I can't just appear in Dublin, barging into other people's lives, lives I know nothing about, and drag Cara out in some grand romantic gesture. It's too complicated for that. I have no right to stand between her and her sick mother. It'd be insensitive and bullish. I may look big but I'm no bully. Her mother has to be her priority right now. Otherwise, she'll live with the regret for a long time to come. If only she realised what a dick Declan is: *I don't like to tell her that I've had so much sex that I've literally lost count of the number of women I've bedded.* The man's deluded as well, believing that Cara is still a virgin. What did he say? That she'd never been touched. *Rather quaint, don't you think — saving herself for me.* If only you knew, mate. If only you knew! But the thought doesn't bring me pleasure for long because I know, long-term, he's won. I can't deny it: I may have won the battle but he's sure as hell won the war.

Tony returns with a round of drinks. 'Here you are, Jack. A pint of Guinness. Get that down you. You'll feel better.'

To be fair, that was the idea — to come here, drink copious amounts of alcohol and try and blot out the pain raging inside me. Tony disappears, wanting to play another game of pool. Mac and Alice are off to play a game of darts, inviting me along. But I decline. I'd rather sit here quietly, nursing my drink. Blondie's Heart of Glass is playing and that keeps me happy for a minute or two.

It's at that moment that I'm aware that someone is sitting next to me. It's her again, the blonde girl, wearing that yellow top again.

'Hello,' she says. She raises her glass of what looks like cider. 'Fancy meeting you here. You look tired. Busy day at the barbers?'

'Something like that.'

'We're not been introduced.' She offers her hand. 'I'm Debbie.'

I take it reluctantly. 'Jack.'

'Hello, Jack. I've just beaten your friend at pool. Tony, I think. Twice.'

'Oh, that was you?'

She leans in. 'I think he didn't like losing to a woman. It hurt his male pride.' I laugh. Poor Tony. 'It didn't help that I pretended I'd hardly ever played before. I lied. I've played loads. He bought me this drink.' She clinks her glass against mine. 'Cheers.'

'Cheers.'

'So Tony works in the same place as you – and that other giant, the one with the pretty girl.'

'Yeah, he's the boss but we're all mates really.'

'So, is it in the job description: must be six foot six or more, have a beard, loads of tattoos and look like an extra in Game of Thrones.'

'There's a fourth member of the team as well. Eoin.'

'Don't tell me, Eoin is five foot one, clean shaven and no tattoos.'

I laugh again.

'Listen, Jack, I hope you don't mind me saying this – but you never look particularly happy whenever I see you.'

'It's a long story.'

'I could help.'

'I doubt it.'

'Try me.'

'How?'

She finishes her drink, drowning it in one. It's quite an impressive sight, to be fair. This girl can drink and she's good at pool. I rather like her. She slams her empty glass on the table, belches delicately, and says, 'Come, follow me, and I'll prove it to you.'

Intrigued, I do follow her as Bruce Springsteen's Born in the USA plays. No one notices me as I slip out of the pub following this woman in yellow.

'My flat's just two minutes away. I live at the top of Charlton Road,' she says.

'Oh really? That's…'

'Yes?'

'Nothing.'

We walk quickly side by side, her heels loud on the pavement, my mind blank. It's a mild night, our shadows long under the streetlamps. 'I know you know Charlton Road, Jack. I've seen you walk past my flat often enough.'

Presently, we turn into Charlton Road. As she said, Debbie lives at the High Street end. Cara lives, or rather lived, at the far end. Part of me thinks I'm being stupid here, that I shouldn't be doing this but another part of me thinks this is just what I need to purge myself of Cara. After all, she left *me*, not the other way round. It was, ultimately, her choice.

Debbie leads me up to her first floor flat. She opens the door and flicks on a light switch, and we're greeted by a pair of cats who abruptly disappear on seeing me. She throws off her shoes. 'I'd offer you a coffee or something but I've got something better in mind. Come…'

She takes me into her bedroom, which is bathed in a warm, yellow light, a poster for Dune on the wall, a Picasso print. I hardly have time to take it in when her lips are on mine, her hand pressed against my chest. How did this happen so fast? It's a nice kiss but… but my mind is whirling, a jumble of confused thoughts flips through my fevered mind. I feel her hand inching down towards my waistband, and I know she's not going to find any joy down there, however hard she kisses me. Yet, I so want to do this, I need to do this, to help me get Cara out of my mind and out of my system. But it's all too fast, too frantic, too much! I push her away, shaking my head.

'No. I'm sorry, I… I can't do this.'

'Jack? She's left you. I know, Jack. Tony told me. She's left you.'

'Yeah, she has. She has. But… but I still love her…'

95

Chapter 20: Cara

I spend a lot of time with my ma. I'm careful not to tire her out, so often I just sit there in a chair, next to her bed, and not talk, just read, or scrolling my phone. She likes it, likes having me nearby, keeping her company. Sometimes I read the newspaper to her. She likes to keep up to date with what's happening in the world. Pa's been doing this for months now. They have such faith, my parents. They never complain or blame anyone or anything for my mother's misfortune. I, on the other hand, want to scream at our God, demanding why is my mother, barely fifty years old, dying? She's too young and it isn't fair.

Funnily enough, since coming back, I've hardly seen Declan. He's too busy with his work. He starts early, finishes late. Even when he's with me, I feel as if he's not. He's always so distracted, always on his phone. Declan is a man who can't ever truly relax. I speak to him and it usually takes him a few seconds to take in what I say. We've certainly not been out since my return. I had hoped, perhaps, a little more fanfare from my husband-to-be but no, apparently not. But he is due to come over later this afternoon. So that's nice of him.

But I have seen lots of Ava. Sometimes she joins me upstairs sitting next to Ma. Ma loves it, having her two daughters together. Ava sits there patting her bump. I feel so happy for her, she looks well. She tells me she's phoned Eoin, telling him to return home for a week or two. He needs to be here. We all need to be here, together, reunited – for the sake of Ma. Ava's words come back to me: *I'm going to help you sort this mess out for once and for all.* But, having said that, she's not mentioned it since, let alone suggest how we're going to broach this delicate subject with our mother.

And while I'm here, I think of Jack. I think of him all the time and it hurts. It hollows me out, leaving me quite breathless at times. I'd ring him but amazingly, we never swapped numbers or bumped phones. I don't know Jack's number; he doesn't know mine. In some ways, it's a relief because what would be the point? I hope he's OK. I hated the way I left him. I think of Eoin working alongside him. I want to ask Eoin how Jack is, perhaps pass a message on, but again, there's no point. The damage has been done.

In terms of the wedding, I've not yet done anything – but I have arranged lots of appointments: a meeting with the mums of the little girls that are to be my bridesmaids, a fitting appointment at the dressmakers, an appointment with Declan with the vicar who's going to marry us, and an appointment with the caterer's. It starts now.

But today, it's far more mundane – I'm helping Pa with the shopping. Pa likes doing the weekly shop in the town's Co-Op. He accepts my help and accepts my financial contribution – it's only fair I pay my own way after all. I won't be moving into Declan's home until after our wedding day so I don't expect to stay at my parents without paying my way. It's a warm-ish day, the sun is out and spring is definitely on its way. I'm helping Pa load the car boot with the shopping bags when I see a vaguely familiar figure crossing the Co-Op's car park, heading into the supermarket. 'Isn't that…'

'What's that, love?'

Was it really him? I have to find out. 'Dad, do you mind waiting for me for a few minutes? There's someone I need to speak to.'

'Sure. Take your time, love. I'll be in the car. But not too long though – those frozen peas shouldn't be left too long in the boot.'

How is it that from now on, whenever I hear the words, frozen peas, I think of my dildo? Poor Darius.

I jog across the car park and back into the shop. I can't see him. He can't be far and he definitely didn't walk back out. I walk the length of the shop, casting my eyes down each aisle. I 've missed him. I go back, more slowly this time, checking each aisle carefully. And yes, there he is, carrying a metal basket, checking out the dairy. I approach him slowly. He's thinner than I remember, his black hair swept to one side, wearing a blue suede jacket that's at least one size too big for him.

He turns towards me, a pack of butter in his hands. He looks up and sees me. It takes him a second or two before his brain connects and he recognises me. 'Cara, shit, hello.' He drops the butter into his otherwise empty basket.

'Hello, Barry.'

'Jesus, what are you doing here?'

'Well, Barry, I saw you so I thought I'd come and say hello, see how you are.'

At least he has the decency to look shameful, the bastard. Flecks of dandruff spot the shoulders of his suede jacket.

'I'm fine, all things considered. I thought you were still in London.'

'Not any more. I've come back for several reasons – because I'm getting married soon. To Declan, remember him? I've come back to help look after my mother, who, I'm sure you remember, is not at all well, and also to make sure my poor sister's OK with her pregnancy after the arsewipe of a boyfriend abandoned her.' That hurt him, I can tell. He looks behind me, to the side, anywhere but at me. He wants to escape this. But I step closer, blocking his way. 'Not a very nice thing to do, was it? Getting your girlfriend up the duff then abandoning her.'

'Well, what would *you* have done?'

'Me? I'd have done the honourable thing, Barry, and stuck by her on account that the child is yours.'

He looks at me properly now, as if I've lost it, and the first piercings of concern prick me. Something's happening here.

'You don't know, do you? You have no idea.'

'What do you mean? No idea about what?'

'Ava hasn't told you?'

'Told me what, Barry?'

'That baby, Ava's baby?' He shakes his head. 'It's not mine.'

My mouth drops open. I didn't expect that. 'You're lying. Of course it's yours. Who else would it be? My sister doesn't sleep around.'

'Doesn't she? No? Have you actually asked Ava? The baby is not mine.' He says the words slowly as if I might not understand. And frankly, I don't. He steps right up to me, his eyes boring into mine. 'I've got *no lead* in my pencil, Cara. Know what I mean? That's why I know, Cara, and that's why I left. Not because I was being *dishonourable* but because your bloody sister slept with another man. It's *her* you should be angry with, not me.'

'I'm sorry. I didn't mean to upset you. But… but if it's not yours, whose is it?' My voice is getting steadily louder.

He shakes his head as if full of pity for me. 'She hasn't told you?' he repeats.

'What? Fucking what hasn't she told me, Barry?' I'm shouting now, people are looking at me, a member of staff in the Co-Op uniform looks as if she's deliberating whether to intervene or not.

He pauses a moment. And then he says it. 'That baby, Cara, is not mine – it's Declan's.'

Chapter 21: Jack

I like an invigorating shower in the morning. Helps me wake up, freshens me up, ready for the day that lies ahead. Normally, I'm in and out within a couple of minutes, but today I stand there, the hot water cascading down me as I rub the shower gel into my chest. That run-in with Debbie last night reminds me of things. Reminds me of all the girlfriends I've had over the years. More than I can remember. I call them girlfriends but they were no more than one or two-night stands. I went out with one girl, Kiara, a gorgeous sleek black girl who wore her hair in braids, for a whole month before I got bored of her and unceremoniously dumped her. I wonder where she is now. I hope she's OK. She deserved a whole lot better than me. But I'm a different man now. Cara has, unwittingly, changed me. The man I was before wouldn't have hesitated having sex with Debbie last night. But I said no to her. The word 'no' has never been part of my vocabulary but last night I said no to Debbie and I saw the hurt and disappointment in her eyes as I backed away from her, shaking my head, saying no, no, no, I can't do this, not while Cara looms so large in my head.

Cara breezed into my life, changed me beyond recognition, then disappeared leaving behind just a faint shadow. Physically, it was as if she'd never been here but my heart is bursting with a love that I know will never be sated.

I need to finish this shower and get to work, but my mind is so full of Cara. I remember our lovemaking, the curves of her body, the feel of my cock inside her silky pussy. I imagine my teeth biting gently on her nipple. I so want to kiss her again, feel her tongue touching mine, the whispers in my ear, the way she screeched and arched her back as I entered her, the pleasure and pain my penis caused her as she took in the full length of my shaft. I have an erection now, standing in the shower, and my balls feel heavy with cum. I take my cock in my hand. I haven't got time for this yet I start pulling on it, the red helmet peeking out from my fist. I murmur Cara's name, remembering the shape and weight of her tits, her wonderfully large nipples. I groan loudly, as I wank harder and faster. I imagine she's in the shower with me, on her knees, the water falling on her, her hair wet, watching me wank, cupping my balls, her mouth open in line with my cock, urging me on. 'Go on,' she whispers. She holds up her breasts for me, and the thought of that hits my groin like a zap of electricity, and I can feel it coming up my shaft, coming rapidly now. 'Cara, Cara.' I cum with Cara's name on my lips, with her image in my head, large dollops of spunk shooting out of me, one after the other. 'Oh God, Cara. Cara, my love, my love…'

*

I get to work late, but no customers have come in yet so it doesn't really matter. Everything is ready for the day: all surfaces and basins and mirrors clean and polished, the floor swept, the float done for the til. Tony, lounging in one of the armchairs, draws on his vape, blowing out large clouds of smoke. Eoin is playing a game on his phone while Mac, always the most erudite among us, is reading a book. I still feel shit but I do feel a little better having released some of that tension that had built up inside me.

The atmosphere is strained, it always is now, ever since I met Cara. Eoin doesn't trust me and it's caused a barrier between us which, in turn, has soured the atmosphere between all of us. We're less the Four Musketeers now than the Four Misery-Guts. But what is he still worried about, why isn't he over it yet? Jeez, his sister is safely far away on the other side of the UK, making whoopee with her knob of a fiancé, Declan, and presumably all loved up. Despite what she said in her brief letter to me, I doubt she does remember me still. I'll already be a distant memory in her mind, like Kiara is in mine.

It's almost ten when finally we get our first customer. He's one of Eoin's regulars, one of the 'shave it all off' brigade. Easy work. Don't know why he doesn't just buy himself a set of clippers and do it himself.

Mac fires up the coffee machine, turns the stereo on, and Tony asks whether I saw the game on TV last night. So, we're off, the day starts. Better late than never.

After such a quiet start, we end up having a really busy day – one customer after another, mostly men we know but always a couple of new ones that come in and see what we're all about. Around half past three, we start to get the mums coming in with their boys. Today, unusually, we even had a young girl in, about twelve years old, wanting a boy cut. I was happy to oblige. Sweet little thing. And her mum was nice, leaving me a good tip, far more than what was necessary.

It's almost six o'clock. It's closing time and it's almost dark out there. It's been a good day. Even Eoin slaps me on the back at one point, asking if I was OK. 'Sure,' I said. 'Thanks for asking, mate.' And I meant it; I was touched.

Alice appears, looking gorgeous as always. She kisses Mac and says hello to the rest of us. Apparently, they're off to that new Italian restaurant they tried recently. Must have been good then if they're heading back so soon.

We're just said our goodbyes, and I'm heading back to my flat, wondering what to have for dinner, when I hear my name being called out. For a horrible moment, I think it's Debbie, and frankly, after last night, she's the last person I want to see. But, huge relief, it isn't Debbie. She runs over, catching me up.

'Hi, Jack. How are you?'

'Fine thanks, Hannah. You?'

'Yeah. Can't complain. Listen, you left your jersey at my place.'

'My jumper? Oh, so that's what happened to it. I wondered where I left it.'

'Come over now and you can collect.'

'No, it's all right. I'm not that bothered. Can't you drop it off at the shop, you pass by every day, didn't you say?'

'Yeah, but not at the moment. I'm working from home for now. So, no, I won't be passing.'

'Oh, don't worry then, just chuck it out.'

'No, Jack, I don't want to do that, it's not right, just chucking out a perfect piece of clothing.'

'It's only a jumper, Hannah.'

'No, it's good wool that.'

'Give it to a charity then if you're that worried.' I can see she's determined here, although why I've no idea. 'OK, OK,' I say, putting my hands up, admitting defeat. 'I give in. I'll pop by some point.'

'No, I mean now, Jack. This minute.'

'Christ, Hannah…'

Chapter 22: Cara

I'm still processing this. Barry can't have children – 'no lead in his pencil', poor man. My 'lovely' older sister, my friend, my mentor, has slept with my fiancé. Christ. What sort of woman does that? I watched Barry saunter off with his shopping basket in the crook of his arm, and I actually felt sorry for the man. What must it feel like, knowing that the woman that you love, the woman you want to marry, is having an affair with a man like Declan. And then, to cap it off, he's gone and impregnated her.

I returned home from the Co-Op, my dad driving the car. He must have seen the steam bowling out of my ears. At one point, he asked if I was OK. 'Fine,' I barked back at him, obvious that I was anything but fine, but he was either wise enough or not brave enough to pursue it. I am fuming, I can barely contain myself. To think I told her everything about how I feel about Declan with no idea that she had bloody slept with him and was expecting *his* baby. Was she laughing at me? Does she love Declan? Was she annoyed that I should be marrying the father of her child? And poor Barry, cast as the villain in this sorry saga. He deserved better than the whore that is my sister.

On arriving home, I storm out of the car, not looking back. I hear Dad say, 'Don't you worry, Cara, I can bring all this shopping by myself.'

I run upstairs, heading for my bedroom when I hear Ava's voice coming from my mother's room. My poor mother. How will she react when she finds out? Because she's going to find, everyone's going to find out, and they're going to find out straight away.

I pop my head around Ma's bedroom door. 'Can I come in?' I ask, all sweetness and light.

'Sure,' says Ava, beckoning me in.

I approach Ma's bed. She smiles on seeing me.

'How are you feeling today, Ma?'

'Oh, not too bad, love. Not too bad. Are we still expecting a visit from Declan today?'

I look at my phone to check the time. 'Yes, any minute now actually.'

'Ava and I were just talking, weren't we, love? Shouldn't you book an appointment with Father O'Malley soon?'

'Already have. Declan and I are seeing him on Friday evening. At least, that was the idea. Might need to cancel that now.' I glance over at Ava. I can see her absorbing this but not responding.

'Well, I hope you don't cancel, love. Time is marching on. Anyway, where have you been this morning?'

I tell her about going into town with Pa, and about doing the big shop in the Co-Op there. My mother smiles and nods her head. 'And then, would you believe it…' I lock eyes with Ava. 'I bumped into Barry of all people.'

Ava pales on hearing her ex-boyfriend's name.

Ma stiffens too. 'Oh, Cara, don't mention that name in my presence.'

'What, the father of your future grandson, Ma?'

'He's no father to this child.'

'Well, ain't that the truth?'

Ava shoots up from her chair. 'What do you mean by that? What did he say to you?'

I stand too so we're both standing on either side of Ma's bed, Ma watching this exchange like a spectator at a tennis match, left, right, left, right. 'I think you know the answer to that,' I say.

'Tell me, Cara. What did he say?'

'You really want me to say? Here? Now?'

She glances down at Ma. 'No, actually I don't.'

'But I do,' says Ma firmly. 'What are you saying, Cara? What did Barry say to you?'

Ava, still standing, is crying now.

'Do you want to tell her, Ava? Or shall I?'

She's breathing heavily, unsure whether I'm bluffing her. 'It wasn't meant to happen,' she says in a whisper.

'What wasn't meant to happen, Ava?'

She looks down at Ma's bed, pulling on her rings. She can't look me in the eye as she confesses. 'Declan and me.'

Ma stares at her, open-mouthed. 'What did you just say, love?'

'I never thought… I just… I didn't mean it to happen, it…'

'What's happened, love? I didn't catch that. Why don't you both sit down, hey? Please, you're making the place look untidy.'

We sit down, both of us. Ava still can't look at me. She presses her fingers into her eyes, trying to stem the flow of tears. 'Tell her, Ava.'

She takes a deep breath and holds it for an age. Finally, she exhales. She's ready. 'Ma, I've got something to tell you, and Pa and Eoin, everyone. But you first. This baby I'm carrying… it's not Barry's.'

'Is it not, love? Well, if it isn't Barry's, whose baby is it then? Do you know?'

'Yes, Ma. I know.' She swallows. 'It's Declan's.' Finally, she throws me a furtive glance and I know it's filled with remorse. But I'm not going to let her off the hook, not yet.

My mother seems to be grappling with this. 'Declan, love? Are you…? I mean… Are you sure? Cara's Declan?'

'Yes, Ma. Cara's Declan.'

'Does he know?'

'Yes, good question, Ava. Does my fiancé know he's fathered my sister's child?'

She nods, her eyes cast down again.

'Oh, great. So I'm guessing you said, "You tell her, Declan." And he said, "No, you tell her, Ava." And somehow between the two of you, you sorta forgot, or assumed the other had done it and told me.'

Ma's breathing heavily. This is too much for her, too big a shock. Shit. Ava too looks worried. We can't say anything more. Ava will look after her, help her calm down and get some sleep. I have to leave before I make things worse. Quietly, I leave the bedroom, gently closing the door behind me, and make my way downstairs. And what do I see in our living room, my father and my *ex*-fiancé sitting in winged-back armchairs having a cosy one-to-one chat.

'That second goal though,' I hear my father say. 'Should never have been disallowed.'

Oh, they're talking football. Bloody typical! Football.

Declan stands on seeing me. 'Oh, hi, baby,' he says

cheerfully. Then he sees the look of thunder on my face. 'Whoa, what's up, baby? What's wrong?'

'You bastard.'

'Eh?'

'What's going on?' says Pa, swivelling around in his chair.

'Cara, baby?' I can see all his thoughts as they trip over themselves in his little, deceiving brain: *she can't possibly know; Ava would never have told her, but she looks like she does know; shit, what do I say here?*

'So, Declan, at what point were you going to tell my father here that you are the father of his first grandchild?'

Declan looks winded, Pa looks utterly bewildered.

'What did you say, love? I didn't catch a word of that.'

'Baby, let me explain—'

'You what? How do you explain something like this away, Declan? No, I don't want to hear it because you know what?' I step closer to him. He steps back, afraid of me. I wrestle my engagement ring off. I always liked the ring, diamonds and sapphire. But still, needs must. 'I'm not fucking interested.' I throw the ring at him.

'Cara!' shouts Pa. 'Stop this. What on earth is going on?'

'Don't ask me, Pa, ask Declan here, your precious future son-in-law. He'll tell you everything, won't you, Declan?'

I turn my back on them and head for the door. But Pa calls after me. 'Cara, where are you going?'

I stop. Without turning around, I tell him. 'I'll be back in a couple of days, Pa. But first there's someone I need to see. Someone who lives in London.'

Chapter 23: Jack

So, I've made the detour via Hannah's flat in order to pick up my jumper yet she still seems unwilling to let me go. 'Have a cup of tea, Jack,' she says, almost forcing me to sit down in the kitchen.

'No, you're alright, Hannah. Thanks anyway.'

'I'll throw in a biscuit.'

'No, it's fine. I'll just–'

'So how's it going at Mac the Clipper? Business good?'

'It's OK.'

She starts telling me about her job at the hair transplant place. I interrupt her. 'I didn't know you worked at the same place as Cara.'

'Didn't she say? Yes, it's how we met. They haven't even started the recruitment process to replace her so theoretically, if Cara returned today, she'd get her old job back.'

I sigh. 'Yes, but it's hardly likely to happen, is it? Can I have a look at her room?'

'Of course. Help yourself.'

Oh, I didn't expect to be so affected by Cara's empty room.

It's just a shell, an empty, echoey shell, what did I expect? But it still feels as if her ghost lingers here. I can detect the faintest whiff of her scent, I can hear her laugh, I can hear that lovely Irish lilt to her voice, I can visualise the sparkle in her eyes, feel the touch of her hand in mine, of her lips on mine. I sit on the end of the bed and run my hand over the bedspread. Oh, Cara, where are you, my love, why, why did you have to leave me? I stand at her window and look down on the quiet street. The streetlamps have come on. I can see the circulating yellow light of a dustbin lorry further down the street. A man stops to bend down and say hello to a little black and white cat on the pavement. For some reason, the gesture tugs at my heart, the simple affection of it. I close the curtains and return to the kitchen.

Hannah has made me that cup of tea even though I hadn't asked for it. 'Do you take sugar?'

I shake my head. 'Has your landlord started advertising for Cara's replacement yet?'

'Landlady. Yes, unfortunately. Actually…' She glances at her watch. 'I'm expecting someone any moment. I said I'd show the girl around. Hopefully, she'll like the place. Can't see why not, it's a nice flat, good location and relatively cheap – for London, that is. You could move in if you want, Jack. Then, if you ever need to… er, have company for–'

'I'm fine where I am thanks.'

'Yes. Of course you are. How's the tea?'

I take a sip. 'Yeah, very nice. Thanks. But listen, thanks for the jumper but I 'd better be going now.'

'No, no, you stay put, Jack. There's no hurry really, is there? Nothing for you to rush home to. If you're hungry, I can rustle up a little something to please your palette.'

I laugh but actually, I can see she's being serious. It's all a little odd. She knows I'm not interested in her in that way so why all this weirdness, this desire to keep me here pinned in her apartment?

'Well, if you're sure.' Her phone pings. She reads her text. 'Oh, Jack, listen, I need to pop out for a couple of minutes. Would you mind staying here in case that girl turns up, the potential flat share girl?'

'Really? Won't she be worried about being alone with a strange man?'

'Nah, I won't be long. She knows that.' She checks her pockets for her phone, grabs a set of keys from a dish on the table and, with a cheery 'won't be long', leaves.

So, here I am – alone in Cara's former flat. It feels all rather odd. I drum my fingers on the table and sip my tea. I check my phone and read a story about a man who tried to kill his wife by tampering with her parachute. I think about downloading one of those dating apps to my phone but the thought of it makes me queasy. I really can't face it, the whole dating game, meeting incompatible woman after incompatible woman, comparing each and every one to Cara, setting a bar so high that not a single one would have any chance of coming anywhere near it. I once had a date with a woman who was an adrenaline junky – she liked doing bungee jumps and the like. She was adventurous in the bedroom too but it was all a bit too much for me, it felt as if she liked experimenting with things and I was her crash test dummy. I could have been anyone. It didn't last long. The time passes. Hannah's taking her time and now I am beginning to get hungry. I'd text her and ask her how much longer but I don't have her number, just as I still don't have Cara's number.

The buzzer rings. Damn it, where is Hannah? She's been ages. I answer. 'Hannah's flat.' But there's no answer. 'Hello?

Hello, is anyone there?' Still no answer, so I hang up and head back to the kitchen.

Two minutes later, there's a knock on the door. Perhaps someone downstairs and let this woman in. I answer the door. 'Fuck!' The expletive leaves my mouth, I stagger back, my heart pounds. 'Cara! What the fuck?'

She grins the biggest smile, she's bouncing on her toes like a child on Christmas morning. There's a suitcase on the floor next to her. 'Hello, Jack.'

'Hannah said that…' Oh my God, it's all beginning to slot into place. She knew. Hannah knew Cara was coming back, that's why she invited me back, that's why she pinned me down with chat and tea, that's why she sneaked out. There is something by the way Cara is looking at me which stirs my heart, the way she's looking at me, her smile. 'You've come back for good, haven't you?'

She takes a moment to answer and the pain is unbearable. My whole fucking life rests on the answer here…

'Yes, Jack,' she says. 'I'm back for good.'

I hear the words but it takes a few seconds to register. And when it does, I scream. I pick her and her suitcase up from the threshold and, spinning around, carry her into the flat. I kick open her bedroom door and throw her on her bed. She sits up, laughing.

'You're truly back for good?' I ask. 'Or are you going back to Ireland?'

'It's up to you, Jack. Would you like me to stay?'

'Would I… Seriously? You're prepared to stay here in London? For good?'

'If you'll have me. Your wish is my command.'

My insides turn to liquid. 'Oh my God.' I cup her face in my hands and kiss her.

'I take that as a yes?'

'Yes, yes and a million times, yes.'

'So you definitely want me to stay?'

'Yes!'

'I want you to prove it to then, Jack. If you can fuck me like never before, I might just believe you. You think you're up to it, Jack? Hmm, up to the challenge?'

'I think we'll see about that…'

I kiss her, my hands running down her back. I lift her arms and hoist her top off. Down to her bra, she makes urgent panting noises as she removes my shirt and runs her fingers down my chest, over my tattoos. Oh, the touch of her fingertips on my flesh causes an almost electric charge down to my cock, and I can feel it rapidly stirring into life. We both squirm out of our jeans, laughing a little, both excited. I touch her warm pussy through the fabric of her panties and my balls ache with desire. I clench my eyes shut, overawed by this woman's beauty. 'Are you OK?' she whispers.

'Cara, seriously, I could come just looking at you.'

'Oh, you big bear, you.'

She removes my cock from its restraint and gasps on seeing it. Holding it by its base, she just stares at me. God, it's so painfully hard, dripping precum from its tip and I'm so worried I might ejaculate now and shoot my load over her face. She whips off her bra and her panties, and my eyes zip from her face to her breasts to her cunt. The word 'fuck' slips from my mouth because I know I've never experienced such desire in my life before. This is something else. She spreads her legs, giving my eyes a feast. My legs almost buckle on seeing her glistening lips. Her fingers creep down and slowly she pulls her labia apart and I let out an involuntary grunt. I run my finger the length of her slit, and, using my thumb, circle the little nub. She lets out a painful cry. Her eyes roll back. I allow my tongue to do the work now, lapping up the sudden appearance of her white juices, tasting her sweetness. Her fingers grip my hair and she pushes my head into her cunt, suffocating me between her legs. Her wetness coats my lips and my moustache as I slabber at her slit, taking joy in hearing her whimper and whine. I lift her an inch so that I can squeeze her ass. I lap greedily on her juices, my fingers pushing into her. Her hips buck and her fingers pull at her hair as she comes, my name on her lips. 'I need you inside me now, Jack.' I creep up the bed, kissing her as I inch up. When, finally, my lips touch hers, I gently guide just my knob into her gaping and all-too ready hole. Her eyes glaze over, her eyelids fluttering. I feel her wet flesh tightening around me, squeezing more precum out of me. I kiss the side of her face, her neck, breathe in the scent of her hair. I'm desperate to pound her but I know I must start gently, probing that cunt, easing myself in, inch by inch. I can feel a trickle sweat running down my back, between my shoulder blades.

'Jesus, Cara, this feels so good, so right, babes.'

She wraps her arms around me, squeezing me tightly to her. 'Give it to me, Jack.'

'You mean like this?' I slam the rest of my cock inside her hard, cruelly hard, and she bucks and screams. I thrust repeatedly. She yelps each time as I hit home. Her legs wrap themselves around me, forcing my hips to grind even deeper into her glorious slick pussy. Her fingernails dig deep into the flesh of my arse. I shut my eyes and bite back the pain but I maintain my frantic rhythm. I know I'm not going to last much longer. Her body quivers beneath mine. We disengage. She manoeuvres herself on the bed and gets down on all fours, facing away from me. My heart skips a beat on seeing her swollen, soaking wet pussy twitching with anticipation. I insert a finger into the black hole in front of me and twist it around and around, making her squeal. Her arse bucks and shudders. She throws her head back, her blonde hair falling onto her back, before sliding off and forming a curtain either side of her face. I can hear her quietly growling. She wriggles her arse and I know that's an invite for me to fuck her now, from behind. But first, unable to resist the temptation, I run my tongue up her slit, laving her juices. Her clitoris is so swollen, so hard. I flick my tongue over it in quick succession and she mewls in almost pained ecstasy. She's so wet that when I come away my beard is soaked by her.

'Give me your cock now, Jack.'

From this angle, I'm more aware of my length. I don't want to hurt her. But she pushes back on me, whimpering slightly as she does so.

'Careful, babes.'

'It's OK,' she grunts as she pushes back, swallowing entirely the full length of my trunk. Gently, I start moving. 'Go on, Jack, I want it harder, much harder.'

So I pump hard, my body slapping against hers. My hands clasp her hips. I catch the side view of her tits jiggling in time with my pounding, which, if possible, turns me on even more, the slapping getting louder, the thrusts faster. Her body starts bucking again and I know she's coming again. Her fingers claw at the sheets as the walls of her cunt tighten around my shaft. She screams as she climaxes. I should slow down a moment, give her a chance to recover, but I can't, I'm too close. Instead, I thrust even harder, my balls slapping against her arse, tightening my grip on her hips, watching her tits jiggling so fast they become a blur. Then, with a deep, guttural roar, I spurt huge amounts of spunk into her hole. It carries on coming, wave after wave. I grunt with each fresh explosion until, finally, there is nothing left of me to give.

Epilogue: Cara

Jack and I are in a cafe called Bertie's on the Holloway Road in North London, not so far from the barbershop. Mac recommended it. It smells deliciously of coffee, chocolate and cinnamon. It's run by a camp guy called George who wears a 1980's style ponytail. It feels rather industrial: brick walls, wooden floor, low-hanging lampshades, movie posters and framed prints of moody Parisian street scenes. Not dissimilar really to Mac the Clipper. Jack takes my hand. He knows how worried I am about this. I look at the menu though I have no intention of eating anything. Just a large and very strong coffee for me.

'It'll be fine, Cara,' says Jack. 'He'll be fine. Stop worrying now.'

'I know. Thanks, Jack.' I don't know why I'm so nervous about this, this is my life, mine and Jack's; it's none of his business. But that's the thing with older siblings, isn't it? Whatever we say, we still crave their acceptance, their permission. The London part of my life has fallen back in place – I managed to get both my old job and my flat back in time. Both were thanks to my bestie, Hannah. What a girl. She's due to join us in a while. I'm hoping she doesn't walk into a frosty atmosphere. And of course, I've got my love life sorted – for now and forever!

Now, I just need to sort out the Irish part of my life, and I'll be one very happy person.

I had intended to return straight to Ireland, not for good this time, but to spend time with Ma, to help look after her. But when Eoin got an agitated phone call from Pa, Eoin went to Ireland instead. And now, he's back in London and I await his report, my heart in my mouth.

And here he is, my big giant of a brother, marching over, unaware that he's captured the attention of the whole cafe.

George comes over in short, quick strides. 'Oh, gentlemen, hullo. Welcome. Oh, and lady,' he adds, bowing at me. 'Let me know when you're ready to order.'

I think the sight of these two burly men, Jack and Eoin, has positively made George's day!

The two men exchange pleasantries.

'So,' I say, unable to endure this a moment longer. 'How did it go?'

'Yeah, well. The shit certainly hit the fan. Jesus wept, you couldn't have made it up.'

'They all hate me, don't they? They blame me for everything that's happened, they think it's all my fault.'

'Have you finished, Cara?' says Eoin. 'Everything's fine.'

'It is?' I glance over at Jack and feel the warmth emanating from him. God, I love him.

'Yeah, everything was in the air for a while but once it fell and settled, well…'

'You all realised it was for the better,' said Jack.

'Yeah, exactly.'

'Really?' I say, the light at the end of the tunnel becoming increasingly more visible.

'Think about it, Cara. Since you called off the wedding, Ava is now with Declan, as in permanently. So Ava's child is going to be born to a happy couple, not a miserable single parent. Barry's got himself a new girlfriend, apparently, and you and Jack are together and, by the looks of it, very much in love.'

Jack and I smile at each other.

Eoin continues. 'And Ma and Pa? Well, it took them a while to readjust, especially Ma, but we talked and I said about how upset can sometimes be a force for change, good change, and she, like Pa, began to see the positives.'

'Oh, Eoin. This is beyond what I dared wished for.'

'Yeah, so you see, I'm not always the grumpy fucker, am I?'

'Shall we order that coffee?' says Jack. 'I don't know about you two, but I could do with one right now.'

'I'll go up to the counter,' says Eoin. 'Order from there.'

Left alone, Jack takes my hand again. 'Happy?'

'I am now.'

'I told you it'd turn out fine.'

'I know.' I can feel my heart slowing down. 'I know. Thank you, Jack. You've come into my life and saved me.'

'And thank you, Cara.'

'Why are you thanking me?'

'Because I spent so many years looking for love but I was doing it wrong. Always trying too hard and looking in the wrong places. You've taught me, Cara, taught me what's right.'

We squeeze hands. 'You and me both, kiddo.'

'Aha, the happy couple!' We look up to see a beaming Hannah. Eoin returns. They greet each other with a kiss. It's only then I notice that Hannah has Patch with her. I screech Patch's name. He wags his tail on seeing me.

'Yep, it's my turn to dog sit.'

I pick him up and put him on my lap. Jack leans over and strokes him. Hannah and Eoin start talking about dogs.

'I know what you're thinking,' whispers Jack.

'Yeah, I know. If it wasn't for this little fellow, we might never have met.'

'I think we should call our firstborn Patch.'

'Hmm, not sure that would work, Jack.'

He laughs. 'I love you, Cara.'

I pat the dog and laugh. 'And I love you, Jack.'

The End

The Barbershop Quartet

The First Cut
The Next Cut
The Deepest Cut
The Final Cut

ARRyder.com

To obtain Ashley's short story / prequel to The Barbershop Quartet, *The Original Cut*, and join his Mailing List and be the first to know of future releases, etc, please go to:

https://www.arryder.com/free-book

9 781838 499327